A DEPT. 6 OPERATION

ZAMIRA SALIEV

A DEPT. 6 OPERATION

ZAMIRA SALIEV

by Valden Bush

2022

BUTTERWORTH BOOKS

Butterworth Books is a different breed of publishing house. It's a home for Indies, for independent authors who take great pride in their work and produce top quality books for readers who deserve the best. Professional editing, professional cover design, professional proof reading, professional book production—you get the idea. As Individual as the Indie authors we're proud to work with, we're Butterworths and we're *different*.

Authors currently publishing with us:

E.V. Bancroft
Valden Bush
Michelle Grubb
Helena Harte
Lee Haven
Karen Klyne
AJ Mason
Ally McGuire
James Merrick
Robyn Nyx
Simon Smalley
Brey Willows

For more information visit www.butterworthbooks.co.uk

Zamira Saliev: A Dept. 6 Operation
© 2022 by Valden Bush. All rights reserved.

This trade paperback original is published by
Butterworth Books, Nottingham, England

"The Beauty of Her Soul" from the anthology, *Love You Like A
Woman*, is reproduced with kind permission from Ocean Cocco.

Cataloging information
ISBN: 978-1-915009-28-9
CREDITS
Editors: Nicci Robinson and Victoria Villaseñor
Cover Design: Nicci Robinson, Global Wordsmiths
Illustration: KC Lylark
Production Design: Global Wordsmiths

Acknowledgements

My writing journey continues apace and my knowledge of the craft grows. Thank you, readers, for believing in me and downloading and reading my last book. It makes my journey as an author rewarding and gives me energy to write more stories.

Nicci Robinson and Victoria Villaseñor deserve the largest thank you possible. They have continued to provide knowledge, support, and suggestions for each step along the way with a large dose of humour and care. They have shown patience with the bloops in my manuscript, which at times have been bad enough to make them smile. I still attend Global Wordsmiths' writing retreats and consider my way forward as a learning journey, continuing to learn as I put Nicci and Victoria's words into practice. I still believe that I could not do this without them.

My personal support bubble continues to be my safe space and gives me inspiration. Thank you, Anne and Isa, for understanding, helping me manoeuvre tricky issues both technical and personal, and generally just being there for me. Thank you, Gill, for being my author wife and all that entails....for the time we spend writing together, discussing plot and our stories, alongside life in general. In particular, thank you for making me laugh.

I will miss Bramble, our sixteen-year-old bundle of feline fur, well known to my Zoom colleagues (particularly her tail). She took an active part in writing much of my doctorate, and a good part of both Nero and this book. Writing will not be quite the same without her.

As always, I couldn't have done this without my wife. She still encourages me, gives words of sound advice, lots of cuddles, and keeps me fed with all those vegetables she grows. I love you.

Dedicated to G

Still flying; the sky is
so blue up here.

CHAPTER ONE

HOW COULD ANYONE SLEEP? Half the passengers had their eyes closed but Zamira was jumping up and down inside. Her legs twitched with the adrenaline and the excitement. The jet engines roared loud and consumed the silence. The hum of multiple conversations was surpassed by two babies announcing their need for lunch. Sleeping through the noise was already impossible, and the air was too warm and stuffy. Zamira had dressed for comfort in a T-shirt and jeans for the eleven-hour journey. She focused the airflow control to give her a cool breeze across her face and drifted into a half-sleep state. She was only disturbed by trolleys bringing drinks and later, the smell of curry as the meal trays were brought around.

Zamira sipped at her small cup of burning hot coffee after she'd just about survived the wretched excuse for dinner. She remembered the oshi palov her mumma made. How she missed that explosion of flavor Mumma managed to give food. There was no comparison to the curry she'd just eaten.

"How are you feeling about the conference now that we're on the way?" Claudine Treego tapped Zamira's leg and laughed. "You can't change your mind. It's too late."

Zamira turned toward her professor and smiled. "How could anyone sleep with all this noise? I'll be wide awake for the entire trip. I'm totally wired," she said. "I can see how some people get anxious and nervous about their first conference, but I'm excited. I get to go somewhere and use that 'new academic voice' you keep telling me about. I can't wait."

She couldn't actually believe the Preventing and Combating Corruption in Government Infrastructure Conference in Tokyo had accepted her paper, or that her university had paid for her flight and accommodation just for the prestige of having a speaker at the conference. Zamira had gotten the independence she'd wanted for the last couple of years. Rural Tarinor wasn't where she pictured living out her life, and she didn't want to spend her life running and hiding because of her father. This was the first big step, and she was doing it on her own merits. Her father hadn't arranged it, not that he could, given that she hadn't seen him since she left Tarinor two years ago. The things that had gone wrong in her life had all been because of him, and she wanted nothing to do with him. She tried to steady her pounding heart. Why did he still have that effect on her?

"Giving your first paper is a moment to treasure. You'll need to be on top of your game." Claudine nudged her. "Well, you are already. You're only two or three months away from completing your studies. You're almost a PhD. Have you had any more thoughts about what you want to do next?"

"I'd like to continue focusing on government corruption and look at more countries. I was thinking of asking you if I'm good enough to stay with you and work as part of your group." Zamira crossed her fingers and said a silent prayer. "Maybe I could take on several PhD students as soon as I had the knowledge."

Claudine seemed happy with Zamira's work. Zamira enjoyed what she was doing, and she loved living in Paris. But she wasn't sure her ideas aligned with Claudine's vision. It was also about funding and media interest. Corruption anywhere created media interest, so Zamira was hopeful.

"Good. I've been hoping you wanted to stay, and I've been planning for it," Claudine said. "We could certainly use you in the group. It's not a done deal; we'll have to convince the money magicians that it will work, but I believe we can do that. So welcome to the group."

"Oh, wow. I hadn't expected such a quick decision. Thank you for your confidence in me, I—"

"Good morning. This is your captain speaking. Please return to your seats and fasten your seatbelts."

Claudine shuffled in her seat, looking for the end of her seatbelt. "I hate it when we have a storm during the flight. It's like being on one of those rides at the funfair that leave my stomach in a mess." As she stood, her book and pillow dropped to the floor. "Clever you, you didn't undo yours at all, did you?"

"No." Zamira pulled at the seatbelt clip to make sure it was good and tight. "I've only ever flown once, so I'm not used to it yet. I'm not looking forward to this storm you're talking about." She took a deep breath and wondered if it would cause electrical discharges in the plane.

"Don't worry. We can talk to each other and take our minds off it. Tell me about the points you're going to make at the conference, and I'll ask some questions."

Zamira nodded. She outlined some of the major points she intended to raise before the steward came around and offered them more coffee. They continued chatting, Zamira getting more confident that she knew what to expect from the questions she was likely to get at the conference.

"This is your captain speaking again. We've received information from the airline that a credible threat has been made to our plane. We're going to land at the nearest airport, which is Denebe. Please don't be alarmed. Once we're on the ground, we'll take any necessary action."

Zamira put her feet flat on the floor and gripped the seat armrest tight. Her body stiffened, and she didn't know how to fight the paralysis that threatened her. She'd flown out of Denebe to gain her independence, and she had no desire to see it again.

"Isn't Denebe in your home country?" Claudine asked.

"Yes," Zamira whispered. "But my father is in exile, and I'm sure I won't be welcome. He was in the government and fought corruption, but we both had to flee when my mother disappeared and both our lives were in danger."

"Ma chérie, I hadn't realized that was why you were in Paris. I can understand your fear. I don't think we'll have to get off the plane. They'll probably just search the luggage. I just hope we get water and can use the toilet." Claudine smiled. "We older ladies need our toilets."

Zamira hoped Claudine was right, and it was nothing to do with her or her father. She was glad of their friendship and that Claudine had tried to make light of it. As the plane came in to land, Zamira's heart pounded in her ears and nausea roiled her stomach. She tried to keep an outward expression that would belie the turmoil beneath. The plane slowed and taxied across the airport, the jet engines reducing just a little. Zamira switched her phone on, but there was no signal.

"This is your captain speaking. Please remain in your seats with seat belts fastened until I signal all clear. Thank you for your patience."

The plane stopped, and there was silence as if a storm had blown out and there was nothing left. The stewards walked along the rows, checking that everyone was still wearing their seatbelt. The external doors opened, letting in warm air and the smell of fuel. A uniformed official from the Tarinor Internal Police entered. He was tall and slim, and his uniform was impeccable from the creases in his trousers, pressed to a knife's edge, to his highly polished boots. He held his hat under his arm and rested his other hand on his pistol, clearly expecting trouble. His hair was short and well cut, and he was clean-shaven. He was probably from one of the internal security divisions such as International Intelligence or Presidential Security. Zamira had met several of those officers when her father worked for the government. But this one didn't seem familiar.

He instructed the stewards to sit. Two casually dressed male passengers from a few rows in front of Zamira stood and moved into the gangway. They looked at the uniformed official and nodded. The woman that had been sitting next to Zamira stood and joined them. Zamira hadn't noticed many details about the woman apart from the fact that she smiled when they first boarded and was reading an English newspaper, *The Times*.

"She's where we expected," the woman said in Tarin.

It became clear to Zamira that she was the reason for the stop. The long arm of the Tarinor government was likely behind this, trying to get at her father. Were they planning to use her like they'd used her mother to quiet him and his anti-government rhetoric? She'd spent her life bowing to the pressure her father was under. Her recent independence had been uplifting, and she clenched her fists at the thought of him bringing her into his world again. "Claudine, if this is what I think it is, they're going to arrest me and take me away. Don't look at the official. I don't want them to think you're involved. I don't want them taking you too."

Claudine grasped Zamira's wrist. "What can I do? How can I help?"

She handed Claudine her phone. "Take this. My password is Eiffel3699. My father is in there under Papa. Please contact him when you have a signal. He's the only person who'll know what to do." Zamira leaned back and took a deep breath as they headed up the aisle, looking directly at her. "They're coming for me. Take a video and get people around us to do the same. It may stop me from disappearing if the media knows they have me. Thank you, Claudine." Zamira stood and raised her hands. "I won't give you any trouble," she said in Tarin.

The official took out a pair of handcuffs and signaled for her to put her hands out in front of her. He attached them, and Zamira wondered if handcuffs had been the first step to her mother's disappearance. There had been no one there to see her capture, but Zamira was on a plane with several hundred passengers. It would be impossible for them to manage. She hated her father for this. She tried hard to control her breathing and not allow them to see her terror.

"We are taking this terrorist off the plane for your safety and will imprison her here in Tarin to await trial," the official said loudly to the passengers and nearby stewards.

Several people held their phones aloft, clearly recording the proceedings. She had a better chance than her mother. Zamira followed her captors out of the plane as people stared at her. She'd done nothing wrong, but some of them looked at her as if she *were* an actual terrorist. She walked a little quicker, needing to get out of there. She emerged from the plane into a sunny morning, and the rest of the world was going about its normal business. This wasn't how her flight to Tokyo was supposed to go. From celebrating attendance at her first major conference and getting a place in her professor's research group to this. She'd worked hard to get there, and now it was all over. What was it they said about pride and a fall? This wasn't a fall; it was an enormous dive. Her legs shook as she went down the steps. The two men grabbed her arms and almost lifted her toward a waiting black limousine.

Zamira glanced over her shoulder at the plane. The doors closed and signaled the end of the life she loved. She bit her lip to hold back the tears. She wouldn't give these people the satisfaction.

The official sitting in the row in front of her with the female guard, nodded to her as their car pulled away. "I'm Kapitan Darab Gulov from the Presidential Security Force. The president asked me to collect you from the plane and take you to the palace. He has questions for you," he said. "Once he has finished with you, he will hand you over to me to arrange your custody. You need to be nice. Understand?"

The two men beside her laughed, and one put his hand on her leg. Zamira forced a smile and pushed his hand away. "I'll be happy to speak to President Bek and answer his questions and highlight my excellent treatment," she said.

One of the men turned in his seat with a small sack in his hand. He placed it over her head with practiced ease. So, this is how it's going to be. Swallowing rapidly to keep down a rising tide of nausea, she closed her eyes and took a deep breath. She could do this. She had to. There was no one else to rely on.

***

It was stuffy, hot, and dark as she sat in the back of the car with the sack over her head. Her wrists ached from where the too-tight handcuffs had stopped a bit of the blood flow to her hands. Tears streamed down her face, and she couldn't control her body shaking. She was on a road to nowhere and, just as with her mother, nothing could save her. She'd hardly lived yet, and there was so much she wanted to do. She had been on her way to a new place to explore and enjoy. There was so much of the world she wanted to see and experience. Her PhD would open doors for her all over the world. Okay, she hadn't gotten it yet, but she'd been on her way. She hadn't been in love, she'd never kissed a woman in the rain, she'd never swum naked. She wanted children. She wanted her mumma back. So many things left undone.

The car slowed, and the car window wound down, squeaking all the way. Even the president's car suffered from this country's car disease. They were difficult to get hold of, spares impossible to find, and their engines and moving parts suffered from one too many make-do repairs.

"Kapitan Darab Gulov with guards and prisoner for the president," someone said.

"Proceed."

The car eventually stopped, and they pulled her from the seat. They hauled her up some steps, scraping her shins, then took the sack from her head. Her wrists burned along with her aching shoulders, and the ache in her bladder signaled its urgency. She turned to the female guard. "I need the restroom."

She nodded and led Zamira by the handcuffs toward a door farther down the long corridor. Zamira struggled to remove her clothing as the guard stared at her. Privacy was clearly too much to expect. She washed her hands as best she could and splashed some water on her face.

They marched her out and along the corridor until they came to a double door. The guards opened it, and Gulov took her arm and thrust her inside. Zamira looked around, and her gaze fell on a white-haired man with a carefully trimmed mustache, dressed in a gray suit with a white shirt and black tie. Bek hadn't changed. She looked around the room, with its thick woolen carpet and dark, highly polished furniture. There was a teapot and a set of cups on a tray at one end of the table, as if Bek believed that a pot of tea made him civilized.

"Well done, Kapitan Gulov. I know who to trust to get things done. Hello, Miss Saliev. Do you remember me?" Bek asked.

She clenched her fists in front of her. "Of course I remember my mother's murderer...and now, my kidnapper."

"Now, now, my dear. I'm merely asking you to stay awhile in Tarinor while we find your father. Please sit, and we can discuss your future. Perhaps a cup of green tea will help settle you." He gestured to the female guard. "Remove her handcuffs."

Zamira sat at the table while he drank tea. It was a surreal element in a dreamlike day. No, it was an ordinary moment in the middle of a nightmare.

"I only need to know where your father is. That's not too difficult a thing to ask," he said.

"Then we're going to have a problem, because I haven't spoken to or seen him since I left Tarinor." And she never wanted to speak to him again.

"He is causing me and my government all sorts of trouble. I want him found. Where is he?" Bek asked, less gently this time.

"I HAVE NO IDEA," Zamira said. "You were clever enough to find me. I would've thought it would be easy to find him. Go snap your fingers at the kapitan."

"Mm. You should be careful what comes out of your lovely mouth while you're here. There are a number of different ways this can go. The least unpleasant option would be for you to tell me where your father is, and I'll keep you here in the palace until he joins us. Then I can release you. Gulov, please inform our guest of the next option."

Gulov stepped forward and saluted. "If you don't tell us where your father is, I will take you somewhere secure until you do. If you behave with the press, I will keep you safe from *admirers* like Darvesh here, who would like to spend time with you. There is likely to be a long queue of men who would like to spend time with you rather than guard you. It will be up to the president and me how safe you will be. There may come a time when you'll wish for us to shoot you like your mother."

Zamira sucked in a breath. This was the first time someone had admitted to her that her mumma had been killed by the government. She wouldn't cry or show weakness in front of these murderers. She would be strong, just as Mumma had taught her. "Why *did* you murder her? She didn't have a political bone in her body." It crossed her mind to pick up the teapot and smash it against Bek's head. "You needed my father to toe the line and not reveal to the world how corrupt you are. You thought that if you killed her, he would behave. But you were wrong." Zamira banged her fist on the table. "Now you have both me and my father angry with you, and me angry with my father. Instead of toeing the line, he left the country and has caused you more headaches than if he'd stayed here. I am innocent, as was my mother, and I promise you that I'll make sure you regret you ever decided to hurt my family."

"You have a press conference in about an hour," Bek said as if he'd heard nothing from her. "And we're going to work on what you're going to tell the world's media. I want you to emphasize that we are taking care of you and that you've been told we'll release you when your father arrives in Tarinor. The broadcast will be live, so they understand I have nothing to hide."

"And if I do this press conference?"

"Gulov will take you somewhere secure, and you'll be safe until your father arrives."

Her earlier anger fizzled out into nothingness, leaving Zamira flat, emotionally wrung out, and fully aware that she held no power here. She would have to take these men at their word, but that didn't mean she believed them. Once the press conference was over, she'd be a target. She hoped and prayed that she would get another one, that Bek would need to show her off more than once. That would be the only thing that might keep her safe.

Bek and Gulov went over her words with her, and she repeated what they wanted her to say until they were happy with it. Gulov took Zamira out into the early evening sun and paraded her on the steps of the palace. The low sun in her eyes made it difficult to see. What she could see was confusing, just a mass of faces with flashing cameras and people calling to her. She'd never been the center of attention before. The media was mostly from surrounding countries, although she spied a couple of European stations.

People shouted questions at her, but she'd been told to say nothing but the practiced script. She wasn't about to risk her life and answer any of them. It was obvious that the recordings of her removal from the plane had gone viral. She expected questions were being asked about when it became permissible to divert planes to kidnap passengers. She hoped that world leaders would complain loudly. Zamira sighed deeply, grateful that the world's media hadn't allowed her to disappear without a trace. They were holding Bek accountable.

She read her prepared speech and assured the media that she'd been told the government would look after her until her father returned to Tarinor. "Please, Papa." It wasn't in her script, but she couldn't say *"I'm so angry with you, please do something. I'm frightened,"* so it would have to do.

When it was over, they went back inside. Bek nodded at Gulov, and the female guard handcuffed her once more.

"I will see you again, Miss Saliev," said Bek. "But it would save us all time if you would just tell us where your father is hiding."

"I really don't know. I've told you; the last time I saw him was before I flew out to Paris two years ago."

"Follow me." Gulov took her arm and led her outdoors to a black car.

Inside, the female guard put a covering over Zamira's head again, and the world disappeared. Her stomach twisted and nausea rose. "May I have a drink of water before we set off, please?" She was putting off the moment which had her believing she was walking over the edge of a cliff, and there was no rescue. The darkness of futility came over her. The female guard removed her head covering and thrust a bottle of water into her hands. She drank and while it didn't change how she felt, she hadn't realized how thirsty she was. She handed the bottle back, and they replaced her head covering.

The car set off, and she leaned back into the seat. She had no idea where she was going, and she had no control over anything now or when she got to their destination. Damn her father. He'd better do something this time.

CHAPTER TWO

FLICK WATCHED THE SECOND hand as it crept around the clockface on the wall of her office. Standard, white-faced clocks in offices broke up Department Six's beige walls, the only decoration in a sea of boring and beige. The day was passing so slowly that she was almost inclined to think that time was moving backward. God, she hated the routine of this work.

"Afternoon, boss, and how is your day going in this bright sunshine?" Alex, her colleague and one of her best friends, asked.

They'd worked together in the Special Reconnaissance Service and after D6 had recruited Flick, Alex had followed. Flick smiled. "How can you be so bright? The London sky is gray, this office is drab, and this office work is deathly dull."

"There's the possibility of a new contract, and I think you should volunteer. It's not the usual rescue of women who've been forced into being sex slaves and drug runners. A plane flying from Paris to Tokyo was told to land at Denebe Airport in Tarinor because of a bomb threat. When they landed, the plane was boarded, and a young woman was removed in handcuffs. There are lots of pics and videos taken by the other passengers. Turns out she's the daughter of Almaz Saliev."

Flick looked at Alex. "Why would we volunteer? Is this a D6 job?"

"Because they've promoted you out of the field, and you're bored. You haven't been out in the real world since Leah died, and it's time."

Alex always told her how she saw it. But Flick hadn't managed to lose those thoughts of Leah and their too-short time together. Alex was lucky; she'd never lost anyone. But she and so many others were quick to advise her about moving on. What did they know about her grief? "But why this woman?"

"Because you've done more jobs in Afghanistan and Pakistan than the rest of us put together. And of the ten languages you speak, Russian and Pashtun are two of them. You know this part of the world better than any of us," Alex said.

Flick wrinkled her nose. Something didn't sound right. "Sounds like it's too small for us. We do larger, government-directed ops. I'm sure the bean counters won't be interested in small fry like this."

"Can you remember Almaz Saliev? He came to our attention when his wife disappeared."

Flick stood and looked at the blank wall, stirring her memories around. "Yeah. There was some talk about women being 'disappeared' in Tarinor. No one could prove anything, and we only had half-truths, so we couldn't act."

"Correct. Saliev spoke out about the deals the Tarinor government were doing with the drug dealers running in the south. They were siphoning off enormous sums of money for their personal fortunes. He had to flee the country, as did his daughter. They've kidnapped her to get to him." She leaned on Flick's desk. "This mission has you written all over it."

"It's still only one woman and these days, the politics just won't allow us to rescue one woman." It was a tempting mission. She had to admit she was bored. Her life had become like a photograph that had been left out in the sun for years, drained of its color and vibrancy. She hadn't seen friends or been able to even think about talking to them. She was going through the motions of living. Maybe it *was* time to move on. Could she find her mojo again after all this time deskbound?

"Okay, boss. Just so you know, the general is on his way over to be updated on my last op. Maybe you can get him to back you," Alex said.

Flick sighed. Edward Moss had been a general back in the day. He ran D6 with bluster and bullshit. His outward appearance with a mop of unruly blond hair and a mustache hid the keen mind and highly intelligent man beneath. She would need to make a sound argument if she wanted to be on her way to rescue this woman. She sighed again and returned to her desk, trying to decide if she wanted to do this rescue and if she did, how she could convince Moss.

A loud cough interrupted her thoughts, and she looked up to see Moss.

"Alex asked me to pop in on my way out. What do you need?"

"Almaz Saliev's daughter has been kidnapped by the Tarinor government. We owe him for all the help he gave us in those two Tarinor ops. I'd like to put together a small team and get her out quickly."

"Bit more low-key than our typical fare." He leaned against the windowsill and looked at her. "We'll need to convince Jeffers. He'll want big results for a minor investment. You know he'll say that one woman isn't worth the risk or the money."

Flick tensed her legs. Her heart beat loudly, nearly deafening her thoughts. Jeffers was an ignorant little man who had no idea about women. The only thing he understood was accounts.

Moss stood and put his hand up. "I can see what you're thinking, Flick. Say no more about Jeffers. I understand. I don't agree with him, but he controls the purse strings."

"Yes, sir. I know the odds are against us. We don't know Tarinor, and that'll make it difficult. In the last year, we've spent more and more rescuing women from the Afghanistan, Pakistan, and Tarinor borders."

"Yes, yes, I know. I'll see what can be done."

"We can do it small, sir. I only need a team of three including me. We'd land in Pakistan."

"You have operational control of the department, but it's difficult politically."

"Thank you for backing me, sir."

"As always, Flick. See you at the Friday briefing," he said and left her office.

She looked at the clock again then out the window at the gray London sky. Perhaps an op in Tarinor would get things moving again. The last two years had been so hard and long, it had seemed like a lifetime. This would give her a chance to decide what to do next. The life she was living had no forward motion. And she'd lost almost all of her confidence. Her phone rang.

"Moss here. We have trouble. Jeffers won't spend any money on your mercy mission. I'm going to see Clarke. Not sure if the minister will help, but it's all we can do."

He hung up without waiting for her response. She replaced the receiver, and her phone rang again immediately.

"Ma'am, there's a Mr. Almaz Saliev here to see you. He says you may be expecting him."

"Ask him to take a seat. I'll be down in a moment."

"Yes, ma'am."

Saliev was undoubtedly coming to plead his daughter's case. D6 could help, but Jeffers was too busy counting money instead of lives. She went down the concrete staircase, slightly ashamed that she couldn't grant his inevitable request for help.

She approached him in the waiting area. "Mr. Saliev, I'm Flick Colonna. We haven't met, but your information has been helpful to my department in the past."

Saliev shook her hand. "Thank you for seeing me."

"Of course. Please, come with me." Flick showed him into a meeting room, closed the door, and motioned to a seat. "How can I help you?"

"I need your help to rescue my daughter. She's in a terrible place, and I just cannot bear to let the Tarinor government hurt her to get at me."

"Why not give yourself up in exchange for her?" Flick asked though she knew exactly why. He was causing a lot of political and financial pain to the Tarinor government, and they would take great pleasure in torturing and killing him.

Saliev shook his head. "Even if I did that, there's no guarantee they would give up my daughter. I promise you that what they'll do to me is nothing like what they'll do to her."

"Is your daughter part of your political plans?" Flick asked.

"My daughter hasn't spoken to me in over two years. She is totally independent of me. Imagine how she must be feeling, plucked from her life in Paris. I'm still dealing with them murdering my wife, and my daughter blames me for that. I can't allow her to die for me too." Saliev stood and paced the room. "But the corruption in Tarinor is widespread. I'm trying to change things politically and make life difficult for their government. I've been working hard and have been successful in getting sanctions against them. That's why they're trying to derail me, and by doing this, they are succeeding. President Bek cannot be allowed to get away with this. So I'm here to make a personal plea. If you're truly grateful for my previous assistance, you'll help me now."

"I've already said I would like to help, but the financial and political influences are currently against our intervention. I need to change their minds, and my boss is working on that right now." Flick smiled.

"I can help," Saliev said. "I have contacts in Tarinor, some who help for love and some for money."

Flick had used plenty of both kinds of those people on previous missions. "I'll do what I can to get the rescue approved. If it's a no, then it will be down to you and the pressure you can put on the minister."

Saliev stopped pacing. "Thank you for considering this. I can only hope that you get permission. Time is moving quickly," he said.

Wasn't it always? "I'll see you out."

She returned to her office and leaned against her desk. As usual, it concerned her that she would take women with her and they could die, leaving wives, husbands, and family bereft and unable to move on. Getting Saliev's daughter out would be risky. *Get the innocent woman out.* Everyone in this job signed up fully aware of the risks, but this woman hadn't signed up for anything. She'd just been born in a turbulent country.

Her thoughts turned to her own loss of her wife. Hardly a day went by without that grief choking her. What Alex thought was a promotion had been a godsend to get Flick out of live action. She wasn't certain she was ready to go back to it, even now.

Alex knocked on her door. Flick blinked away her tears before she looked up.

"I'm glad you're still here. Jeffers is in a meeting with the general and the minister in the general's office, telling them they can't have the money I expect."

Her rage lit like the blue touch paper on a firework. Flick didn't speak but was out of her office and outside Moss's in moments. She didn't knock and went straight in. "You're talking about Tarinor and no doubt, Mr. Jeffers doesn't want to pay. It's not good enough." Government bean counters had no idea about what she and her colleagues did, what risks they took in their work. It wasn't for them to make such important life or death situations. "Since when has an innocent woman's life meant so little, particularly when her father has risked his life to help us with our missions? This is exactly the kind of mission the department was created to do: to help any woman in peril using forces outside normal channels. Now Mr. Jeffers is telling us we can't do it because the reward to investment ratio isn't great enough? I'm embarrassed." Flick sat in a chair and waited for their response.

"I think that summarizes things succinctly, Ms. Colonna," Clarke said. "You're absolutely correct that we should commit to this operation. The rescue will go ahead. Now, if you don't mind, I'd like a moment with Ms. Colonna."

Once Moss and Jeffers had left, Clarke turned to Flick. "I haven't seen you for a while. I ran into your parents last week when they were in London. Your father was discussing his new horses. How are you these days?"

Flick had known Clarke since she was a child running around on her parents' estate in nappies. He wasn't a relation, but she'd always called him Uncle Noel. In the office with the presence of others, she called him sir though. "You didn't make the mistake of discussing horse breeding, did you?"

He rolled his eyes. "I did. Luckily, your mother rescued me by introducing her brother, Count Guiseppe, over from Italy. Good save."

"My mother has rescued many people over the years, sir." Flick laughed and rested her arms on the table. "Thank you for helping me organize a different kind of rescue."

Uncle Noel nodded. "Almaz Saliev has been working closely with the government in the UK to bring about change in Tarinor. We've provided him with a base and facilities to help him. The Foreign Office has been grateful for his help with incidents in the border areas between Pakistan, Afghanistan, and Tarinor. We owe him." He sighed. "I hope you're able to rescue Zamira."

He looked directly into her eyes, and his bushy eyebrows made her think of his Labrador, Jess, somehow adorable and cuddly.

"After he fled Tarinor, he secretly came to London while Zamira went to Paris. They've had no contact since. She blames him for her mother's death, and he's stayed away from her to keep her safe."

"I understand, sir," she said and stood, eager to get going. "Mr. Saliev came to see me earlier to ask for our help. My number two reminded me I need to get back into the field, and I have experience in the surrounding countries. I want to do it." She pushed down her misgivings about the possible loss of life.

Uncle Noel came around from his chair. "I know you'll give it your best shot, but be careful, Flick."

"I'll start planning," she said. "I'll send the details through once they're firm."

He put his arm over her shoulder and walked her to the door. "Thank you, my dear."

"Just wish me luck. It's not going to be easy. Those mountains and the people in them are killers."

"With your experience, you don't need luck."

Suitably buoyed, she left and returned to her office, meeting with Alex en route. "Come on, Alex. Get your jacket. We need to eat before I work you all night."

"Oh, good, I'm starving," Alex said, already on her way to the door.

"It's been an unusual afternoon. First you, then the general, then Almaz Saliev, and finally, I gatecrashed the minister's meeting. This woman is special to a lot of people," Flick said.

"It beats watching your clock all day and being miserable," Alex said.

Flick had to admit she'd felt more alive this afternoon than she had for months, but she was working hard to quell the nagging doubts that she might not be up to the task.

***

Flick looked out of the large casement window as the sun came up over the roof of the building opposite and left a dark silhouette of roofline and chimneys. Her planning was almost finished. She just needed to contact prospective team members and put it into motion. It had been much easier with Alex helping to contact all the third parties that went into putting such a complex strategy together. Luckily, they'd done this many times before. They identified and booked the transport route from Brize Norton to Islamabad and put in a request for a Special Ops helo to the LZ once they'd worked out the plan for getting in and out of Tarinor. Ideally, a helo would drop them and pick them up just over the border in Tarinor, although that was the area of the greatest risk. The Tarinor border was known to be particularly lawless in a zone where there were no laws. There were also a number of border checkpoints. Flick decided the higher mountain passes that would miss the checkpoints would be too dangerous as most of them were still snow-covered. They would likely use a checkpoint if they needed to make an emergency exit.

Flick talked to her contacts in Joint Services and managed to obtain some of the latest maps of southern Tarinor to help identify routes to the interior. They didn't know where the woman was being held yet, but they had to have options depending on the circumstances. It meant that Flick had to learn the terrain as quickly as possible, and Alex double-checked her thinking as she identified the variables. What if they had injuries?

What if they were being chased and were forced in a different direction? What would they do if they couldn't find the woman?

They also needed weapons and explosives for a small team. Alex contacted the D6 operations team and ordered what they needed to be waiting for them in Islamabad. In addition, they would need water, some local food, and the means to cook anything they managed to catch if they were in the mountains.

There was a restricted knowledge and access center at the airport, used by Special Ops from the US and UK, which would serve them as a collection point. She requested space for the team. The final point they discussed was the size and makeup of the team. Flick was adamant that it should remain small to be more flexible, just three members including her. They would have to dress as mountain tribesmen to look like a group of shepherds or drug smugglers. Alex wanted a bigger team in uniform, with bigger weapons and a larger footprint to make a statement to President Bek that the Salievs had friends. But Flick held out for a small team that would go in and out quickly and quietly.

In under twelve hours they'd worked out how it would be possible to rescue Zamira Saliev. Flick had played re-runs of all the phone recordings, studied the photos from the kidnapping and the media recordings from the presidential palace. She knew that Darab Gulov was running the operation from their side. She'd heard of him in her army days as an up-and-coming ambitious officer. He'd obviously risen quickly to become the president's right-hand man. Flick had recognized him in the footage of a black car leaving after the press conference with Zamira inside. The last piece of the puzzle was where she was going to be held.

Alex came in with her hands full. "Your favorite, with a sweet and fruity pain au raisin for you, and a cappuccino with a pain au chocolat for me."

"That's likely to be my last espresso for a few days. I'll be at Brize Norton this afternoon and Islamabad tomorrow. I'm expecting Saliev to let me know later this morning what his spies in Tarinor have found out about where Zamira is being held," she said. She took a sip from her steaming drink then looked up. "Thanks, Alex."

Alex sat on the windowsill and looked at their plans. "I'm worried that a three-woman team won't be enough."

"I get that. But in those mountains, we'll be able to blend in more easily than a larger group. If I can get Slim and Chalky, I'll have an explosives expert and a sniper. That's all I need. They may not have the language skills, but both have enough Russian to survive, and I'll do most of the talking." Flick had worked with them closely over the years. Katy White, aka Chalky, had been with her when she first started in the Army and later in the SRS. She was a private contractor now and often worked with D6. Likewise Slim. She was a tiny former army sniper and a deadly Tae-kwon-do black belt who'd been recruited by the SRS before becoming a contractor. They'd worked on more than a dozen ops together, and Flick felt secure, knowing she had people she could rely on.

Alex stood and bent to touch her toes. "I'm stiffening up. What else do you need from me?"

"Nothing. Go home. I'll contact the team, and we'll be set. I'll see you when we get back." Flick moved around her desk and gave Alex a hug. "Thanks for being such a good friend and looking out for me."

"See you in a few days. Good luck with Zamira Saliev. She's gorgeous, so mind what you're doing in those mountains." Alex laughed as she disappeared down the hallway.

Alex was just messing with her head again, another hint that it was time for Flick to move on. Flick was beginning to think that maybe she should, and Zamira was certainly an attractive woman, in a completely different way to Leah. But Flick still woke every morning and felt the stab of aloneness without Leah. She needed all her thoughts to be focused on this op. Flick could worry about her future when she was back in the UK with her team *and* Zamira Saliev.

***

Flick contacted Chalky and Slim before she left her office and confirmed the op was a go. Before she could leave, her phone rang. "Colonna speaking."

"Hello. It's Almaz Saliev. I'm calling to thank you. General Moss called and told me you are a go."

"No problem. We're set to ship out later today."

"I've been given information about Zamira by one of my contacts in Tarinor. She's been taken to the women's prison in Sayeb."

Flick's heart sank. The only women's prison in the country had a good reputation, *officially*. Women were given lessons in basic reading and writing and encouraged to learn to cook. Foreign dignitaries had been to look at how the prison conducted itself, and articles about it had been published. However, behind the scenes was a different story. Most of the women's families wanted nothing to do with them. They had no future and were shunned by most men the moment they became criminals. Effectively, they were considered non-persons and as such, the all-female guard ranks could do what they wanted with them, including renting them out for sex with men. The *unofficial* reputation of the prison was tragic.

"We'll get her out as soon as we can, sir. I expect the media interest will keep her safe," Flick said, more in hope than knowledge.

"I've arranged a contact at the prison: Lily Sharapova. I cannot guarantee her reliability one hundred percent, but she will take a large dollar cash sum in return for helping you. I worry she'll ask for more money than we have. She's saving to get out of Tarinor."

"Mm. It's a high-risk escape when the attention will be on the prison. Can you offer her something that pays her for results and allows her to leave as well?"

There was silence for a moment. "I suspect that help with a visa and a job could do it. Perhaps adding a plane ticket for success. I hope that'll be good enough," Almaz said. "She'll be in the bar of the Hotel Atlas in Sayeb most nights from nine p.m."

"And I hope we won't have to use her." With the firepower they were taking and the quiet insertion planned, she'd have no need of an unreliable insider. "We'll talk soon when I'm back with your daughter."

"Good luck, Ms. Colonna."

Flick ended the call. She'd hoped for some better news. If Zamira was being held in a private house, it would've been a much easier rescue. Holding her in the prison was a clever idea as far as presidential security was concerned but much more difficult for her team. She was also hoping that the media attention would keep Zamira safe. They'd have to move as quickly as possible to ensure her safety in the prison. She located a copy of the prison layout from the office file. She studied the plans for a while before deciding that the kitchens would be the ideal place for an armed rescue.

She left her office and headed to a little-known set of tunnels in a basement beneath Whitehall, where she was given male Tarin clothing for Chalky, Slim, and herself. All three of them were androgynous, which would make it easier for them to be successful in crossing the borders around Afghanistan. They would pick up everything else they needed when they landed in Pakistan.

She arrived at Brize Norton at three in the afternoon, a few hours before her flight to Pakistan. She hadn't managed to get any sleep. It was always the same pre-op. Even if she did sleep, it was restlessly, living the plans in her head, looking at contingencies, working out what would happen if things changed. She entered the flight terminal, and before she could put down her kitbag, she was engulfed by a pair of arms. At six and a half feet tall, Chalky had five inches over Flick.

"I don't know why I think you're my friend. You never call or email, and I don't get to see you any more...well, not since Leah."

Flick's emotions roiled inside her: pleasure at seeing her old friend again and guilt for not being in touch with her sooner. "It's been hard since Leah passed and as each week went by, it got harder." But now she was at least *thinking* about starting to look forward, and maybe the worst of her grieving *was* over.

"I understand that you've been grieving, but so was I. Leah was my friend, and I needed you too." Chalky ran her hand through her hair then shrugged. "I'll forgive you now that you've finally gotten in touch. But after this, I'll haunt you if you don't let me talk to you."

Flick held Chalky's arms. "I've been in a dark place, and I didn't want anyone there with me. Once we find Slim, you can tell me about what you've been up to. I assume Slim is here somewhere," she said.

"We've set up camp over there by the vending machine. As per instructions, we have nothing with us, and we're wearing clothing that can be ditched. In the two years since you've seen us, Slim hasn't grown any. She still looks about eleven. Though compared to us, she should be Shorty, not Slim," Chalky said and motioned toward Slim.

They walked toward her. Chalky hadn't lied about Slim's appearance, but it was a good thing. Once she was in Tarin clothing, Slim would look like a teenage boy.

"Flick. Good to see you," Slim said.

"And you. I'm glad you were both free. It'll be good to get the old team back together again. We'll have to get the beers in when we get back. No time for it now." Flick shook off the feeling of chatting to Chalky and Slim as easily as she would have in the past. So much had happened since they'd seen each other at Leah's funeral.

"It's good to be together again. We'll hold you to that drink," Chalky said.

"Yep. Life is suddenly looking better," Slim said.

"Okay, old friends. They've set aside a room for us. I need to brief you about the op." Flick picked up her kitbag and looked at her watch. "We'll grab some food after the briefing, and then it'll be time for our flight."

They boarded a routine forces flight to Islamabad that carried only a few passengers, all dressed in civilian clothes like themselves, and packed up with a huge amount of military equipment. The seats were just netting over metal frames, made to carry large numbers of troops and their kit to deployments. Comfort wasn't a consideration.

Despite being used to this sort of travel, seven hours on military transport wasn't something that Flick enjoyed. The flight was really noisy, and they wore earplugs which didn't cut out that much sound. There was little inside the plane to allow for passenger luxury, and the toilet had only a shabbily hung blanket as a privacy curtain. She was used to being in charge of an op, but this was the first in over two years, and her nerves jangled dangerously close to her skin. It would be fine, but she couldn't wait to get on the ground and get moving. She lay down across some seats and tried to get some rest. She tugged an army issue blanket over herself, but it did little to combat the chill. She would've been a lot happier with a few hot drinks instead of a packed lunch and a can of soda. Used to far worse than this, she drifted into a light sleep.

The captain's instruction to strap in for landing woke her. Chalky and Slim looked disheveled, and she expected she didn't fare much better. They were more like street beggars than the cream of the UK's special operations' teams.

Once they'd landed in Islamabad, they were met by a woman who introduced herself as Fitz. She led them to a battered brown car and drove them out to a building on the far side of the airfield. The building had few windows, and there were a number of nondescript vehicles parked outside. A couple of hundred yards from the building was a small hangar. Flick guessed they belonged to the Special Ops teams and that the hangar housed their helos.

They left the car, and Fitz led them to a side door. "You're expected," she said, beckoning them in. "I'm your pilot. We have a few hours before we leave."

"Good to meet you, Fitz. I have the co-ordinates for our landing spot and details of our pickup. Who do I give them to?"

"I'll fix it. The less people you meet, the better. There's a room here for you. Follow me."

Fitz led them along a corridor with a lot of closed metal doors and a red painted floor. She opened one of the doors and ushered them into an empty room.

"The list of things you ordered is there on the table. Please double check it. There's a small crate of weapons in the corner. The ammo and explosives are next to it. The food and water containers are on the table," Fitz said.

Flick walked across the room and picked up the list. "Thank you. I'll check now. How do I contact you?"

"If you need anything, press the red button on that phone." Fitz headed toward the door. "Get ready for departure in four hours. Anything that's left behind will be disposed of." She indicated a machine in the corner. "Tea, coffee, and chocolate are over there. I'll bring a hot meal in a couple of hours. Please don't leave this room. This building is used by a number of agencies, and we all try to keep ourselves private and secure." Fitz turned and left.

"What is this place?" Slim asked. "I've been holed up in some strange places, but this is something else."

"I'm not sure myself, but the word at D6 is that it is being used as a conduit to rescue at-risk people from Afghanistan. Hence, no information."

Chalky had already opened the weapons crate. "Lots of serious toys in here. Let's get changed and kitted up before she comes back with food."

They changed into the kit Flick had brought from London. Flick wore a beige knee-length outer shirt with brown drawstring trousers, a brown waistcoat, and an olive-colored blanket over one shoulder. She donned a traditional cap with a turban wrapped around it that hung down over one ear. Her boots were brown leather and well-worn which, along with her sunglasses, were things that showed status for Tarin men. Her cloth bag contained some food wrapped in paper, two water bottles, and forged ID papers for both her and Zamira Saliev. She hid a burner phone for the retrieval op in an internal pocket. Slim and Chalky were similarly dressed.

After they were prepped, the team were taken out of the building to a Black Hawk helicopter. Slim slipped into the co-pilot's seat beside Fitz, and Flick climbed in the back with Chalky. Fitz started the engine and set off toward Tarinor. The crisp autumn morning made the mountains in the near distance look picture-postcard perfect, with the higher range covered in snow. She blew out a long, slow breath. Picture-postcard perfect was how Flick had described her life two and a half years ago. At the top of her game, an expert in her work, and regularly rescuing women from all over the world, she had a wife that she loved and adored with a passion. That postcard went up in flames the day Leah was killed on duty in Afghanistan. Flick hadn't done an op since. She pushed away the fear that she was too rusty to be effective.

The adrenaline rushed around her body, caused by a mixture of fear and anticipation. Fear was a necessary tool. She was experienced enough to be able to control it and use it to energize her. She continued going over her plans in her head while they passed over the terrain below.

Fitz turned the helo as they came to a mountain range and started to follow alongside. "We should be landing in about twenty minutes," she said.

Flick caught sight of a flash on the hillside below her. Milliseconds later, before she could do or say anything, the missile exploded on the nose of the helo. Someone screamed. Was it her? Maybe it was Chalky. The front of their chopper had disappeared, and the wind and sand blasted across her face, stinging her eyes. Chalky groaned, but Flick couldn't see her. Everyone had disappeared. The smell of burning plastic invaded her nostrils, and their bird began to lose height.

Her stomach lurched as they hurtled toward the earth. Pieces of glass, metal, and equipment packs hurtled through the air around her. Flick closed her eyes, put her head between her knees, and her hands over her head. *I'll be with you soon, Leah.* She braced for impact, for the end.

She awoke with her body suspended in the air and resting on top of something hard. She worked out it was the upturned section of the helicopter she'd been sitting in with Chalky, now totally separate from the rest of the charred remains she saw a few meters away. She checked her body. No signs of serious damage, though she had the mother of all headaches. *My team.* She unfastened her still attached seat belt and slid to the ground. Her legs just about functioned as she stumbled across to the remains of the cab. She tried to pull in deep lungfuls of air through her aching chest. The cab of the helo had taken the brunt of the blast and was severely damaged. She blinked against the vision of the remains of her friends in each of the seats, but she was unable to identify them. Body parts were littered around outside of the helo, and she dry-retched. The smell of charred, burning flesh made her heave again. Slim and Fitz were dead. Their part of the helo had taken the brunt of the explosion. Her mind somersaulted into the past. Leah had died in an explosion; had it looked like this? She gagged again. She couldn't go there. She focused and spent several minutes working to ground herself.

Where was Chalky? She crawled through the cab and out the other side to find her friend pinioned between the helo and a rock outfall. She clenched her fists and groaned. Not Chalky. Please God, not Chalky. She couldn't see the bottom half of her body, but a large pool of blood ebbed from beneath her, and she was deathly pale.

Chalky opened her eyes. "Oh, there you are."

"Oh, shit."

"When your time's up your time is up," Chalky said, her breathing labored.

"Shut that talk down right now," Flick said.

"You got any chocolate?"

"Let's get you out of there and then you can have chocolate," Flick said.

Chalky shook her head. "Just give me the chocolate. Don't look at anything below my chest. I'm certain there isn't much left. Looks like I have an appointment to see Leah before you, buddy. I'll give her your love." Chalky closed her eyes for a moment, her face pale and almost ghost-like. She breathed in loudly. "Make it worth it, Flick. Get me a gun and some spare mags, grab what you can from what's left, and go get the woman. You need to leave before the Taliban get here."

Flick acknowledged the spark of envy that Chalky would see Leah before her. She bent over and pressed her forehead to Chalky's. "Yeah, buddy. Give Leah my love. I'll be with you both before you know it, and we can have the party to end all parties." She closed her eyes and took a deep breath but didn't try to stop the tears running down her face. Chalky was right; she had to move. Whoever had shot them down would be there soon, and she needed to be gone. She picked up a water bottle from the ground, all the guns and ammunition she could find, and shoved them into her bag. She also found a bar of Cadbury's. She stopped at Chalky and gave her the chocolate, an L85 rifle, ammo, and a pistol in case she needed it for herself.

"It's been a blast, buddy. Now go. Quickly," Chalky said quietly.

"Be at peace, my friend." Flick set off without looking back, putting one foot in front of the other like an automaton. The urge to lay down and cry pulled at her legs, but she kept moving. She needed to get some distance between her and the helo and head in the opposite direction to whoever had brought them down. She hiked higher up the valley and followed a goat path, working her way northeast and toward Sayeb and the women's prison. Flashes of Slim's body crossed her vision. She blinked them away, along with the tears. She could see her beautiful Leah being mutilated in the same way. Her focus began to slip. She stopped and took a moment to register her body. The ache, the bruising not yet showing, her sore neck. It brought her back into the present. Concentration was key, or she'd never free Zamira Saliev.

There was a checkpoint ahead. She could keep to their basic story and get across the border if she told them she was herding goats and they'd gone high. Pakistan wouldn't care. Tarinor might, but she suspected they were used to herders moving across the border. The checkpoint on the return could be risky, especially if they were being chased. She would work something out for the return. Without Chalky and Slim, a firefight wasn't a good idea. Returning using the mountain route to Pakistan was definitely out of the question.

Being thrown into doing this without her team would be challenging. But she was an expert. She'd been doing ops like this for years and despite all sorts of problems and issues, she'd always succeeded. She may be rusty, but this was like riding a bike. A little wobble and she'd be on her way.

She couldn't afford to think that she'd made a mistake coming back into the field after so long out. It was too late to start second-guessing herself. If she survived this, maybe she should retire completely. Then she wouldn't be tempted into another risky rescue just because she was bored with watching the office clock tick by the hours on her life.

Men's voices in the distance above her filtered into her consciousness. They sounded as if they were coming toward her. She looked around for cover and slid into a small crevasse between some rocks. There wasn't quite enough room to hide her whole body, but it was her only option. Her weapons dug into her side but better being in pain and alive than being like Slim. She gritted her teeth and controlled her breathing until it was shallow and silent. The voices had gotten closer, and she could hear them discussing what they might find; they were hoping for extra weapons and maybe some food.

She managed to sneak a look after they'd passed. They looked like tribesmen, but Flick figured they were probably drug runners looking for anything that would make them money. She counted seven of them, two of which were small boys who looked younger than ten. It was common practice to train young boys to kill and move drugs around the country, and her seeing them armed with guns that looked almost too big for their little hands made it even less acceptable to her. It was one of those things she was powerless to change but was nonetheless upsetting. One of the men had a US-issue rocket launcher over his shoulder. US weapons like that had been seized by tribal groups as they ran drugs between Afghanistan along the borders. But for one to be used against them was sobering. The group were in a hurry to get to their treasure trove, but they'd get a shock when they met Chalky. She'd take as many of them down with her as she could.

Flick moved as soon as the group were gone. She had to hope they wouldn't work out anyone was missing from the helo, but she wasn't injured so there'd be no blood trail for them to follow. Within a few minutes, the silence was broken by the sound of an L85 firing in a long burst. Chalky's last stand. Other shots fired until there was nothing. Flick was the only one left. She stopped walking and looked up at the bright sky, littered with small, white cotton wool ball clouds floating across it. "See you later, Chalky," she said. She may have been alone, but she wanted the message to get to those clouds.

Flick put her head down and started the walk to the checkpoint and the long walk to Sayeb, knowing that the price they'd paid to rescue this woman was already far too high.

CHAPTER THREE

ZAMIRA AWOKE AS THE car engine cut off. It had been a long and tiring journey, and with her head still in a sack, disorienting and claustrophobic. Her head started complaining after a few miles and the pain kept her awake. Someone removed the head covering and handcuffs, and Zamira was pulled out of the car. She took in her surroundings. She was a long way from the Eiffel Tower. The car had stopped in a concrete pull-in, penned in on three sides with walls ten feet high. She tried not to inhale the smell of disinfectant and raw sewage too deeply. An unpainted, battered metal door was pulled across behind her by a woman in a black uniform, sealing off any thought of a quick escape. This had to be Sayeb, the only women's prison in Tarinor. She shuddered.

She knew all about this place. Her father had come home a few years before Zamira left, angry and shouting to her mother about the government. Not unusual, but he was almost crying with the rage. Zamira tried to keep herself in check as images of what might happen to her here ran through her mind. Mostly, her worry was the complete loss of control that she was about to experience. She'd fought hard to get independence in her life. She tried not to tremble and forced herself to remain calm. Gulov might end up being right; perhaps there would come a time when she might wish she'd been shot rather than endure this hell.

"Come with me, Ms. Saliev," Gulov said.

He gestured to the female guard to accompany them. They pulled her toward a black metal door in front of them. It opened automatically, and Zamira suspected they were being watched on camera.

"Good morning, madam. I have our special guest for you," Gulov said to someone she couldn't see.

A woman dressed in a mix of Tarin and Western clothing stepped in front of her. "You are Zamira Saliev?" she asked, and Zamira nodded. "I am Olga Rozakov. I run this facility for the government. You behave as we need, and you will be well treated."

She turned and opened the outside door again. Gulov and the female guard left. Rozakov looked at her, and Zamira took a big breath. As much as she'd hated them and their treatment of her in the last twenty-four hours, they were her only link with the plane and her previous life. She was now on a journey into the unknown. She shivered and tried to make sense of feeling completely divorced from her normal life in Paris.

"Go with the guards. You will be washed, reclothed, and fed. You will find your place here," Rozakov said.

Tarinor was poor and had lived through many years with Russian intervention. Now, corruption ensured that the ruling class lived the life of wealthy magnates. But the past scorn of the decadent ways of Western Europe still prevailed.

Two guards stood behind her. "Move. Follow the red arrows on the floor," one of them said.

They prodded her down the corridor. The floor, walls, and ceiling were raw concrete. The grayness was broken by black doors at regular intervals. Time slowed. This was the beginning of resignation and hopelessness. The floor was damp and smelled of institutional disinfectant. Zamira wrinkled her nose. This was her life now. At another black metal door, she stopped. The door opened, and the guards pushed her toward the counter in front of her. A tall, woman with a pointed nose and short, graying hair was behind the counter. She had sunken dark eyes, and her features reminded Zamira of a wolverine. She hoped she wasn't as vicious.

"Remove all your clothing including any undergarments," she said in Tarin with a Russian accent.

She'd probably stayed behind when the Russians left, happy with her life in Tarinor and not wanting to return to the motherland. She was undoubtedly getting money and other benefits from using the inmates that she wouldn't be able to get back home.

Zamira wrapped her arms around her body. "No. No, I can't."

"You are going to have to learn the rules like everyone else. One, you always do whatever you are told by a guard. Two, you do not speak to guards. Ever. If you disobey, we use these shock sticks to demonstrate we mean it," the wolverine woman said.

One of the guards from behind her circled around and waved a short, metal rod at Zamira. "Remove all your clothing now. Do not make me use this."

Zamira remained frozen to the spot. It felt like she was in a cheap movie. The second guard smiled and nodded, but it wasn't a friendly smile. It was the kind of smile that signified "Don't do what you're told; I'll get pleasure from your disobedience." Yet again Zamira couldn't make a stand. She'd already realized in the presidential palace that her importance would soon disappear once the media lost interest. She needed to play their game. She'd never stripped her clothing off publicly. Even at school, it hadn't been encouraged. She trembled and couldn't stop the tears from forming in her eyes. She began to remove her clothing until she stood naked but for her underwear.

"All of it. Now," the guard behind the counter said.

Zamira removed her final vestige of dignity and shut her eyes. If she couldn't see, she could imagine she was still fully clothed. She stood in the cold concrete room, a chill racing down her spine as she awaited the next degrading instruction.

"As a special prisoner, you may keep your jewelry, and your clothes will be returned to you once they are clean. In the meantime, you will wear prison clothes. You will go into the shower and clean yourself. Everywhere. We will watch. I will examine you and make sure you aren't bringing drugs or any other contraband into the prison." She pulled a bar of soap from behind the counter and threw it at Zamira.

Zamira caught it, and the stench of bleach and disinfectant turned her stomach. The two guards ushered her to the doorless shower cubicle. The water was warm, and the rough soap grated against her skin, like it was removing the top layer. The guards continued to watch her, and she eventually had to wash between her legs. *Rise above this. Don't let them get to me. If I do, they will have won. I need to maintain my dignity.*

The water in the shower stopped, and she was handed a small towel. While she was drying herself, a draft of cold air blew across her back. She looked up to see Rozakov. Of course, she would want to get in on the act. She had nothing left, but it looked like they were about to remove the final shreds of her dignity, piece by piece.

"Come, child. Get your new clothes on. I'll take you to your accommodations. You'll just be in time for some food," Rozakov said.

"Am I allowed to speak to you, madam?" Zamira asked. Would she get a prod with one of those sticks? She was breaking the "No speaking to the guards" rule already and wasn't sure if she'd be in trouble.

"Yes, of course," Rozakov said.

"We haven't checked her for contraband yet," the wolverine woman said.

"There's no need. Just get dressed, Ms. Saliev."

Zamira put on the shapeless clothing that was given her and finally stood in front of Rozakov. "Thank you for your help and kindness," she said.

Rozakov took her into the central prison building. The main prison hall contained women busy sewing, cleaning, and supervising children. Groups of children were scattered across the room, some running around and playing chase. Zamira caught a glimpse into the kitchen where they were preparing meals.

"You are welcome in this part of the prison, but I have given you a room in the east wing which houses our older ladies, the medical center, and the library. It is quieter. I am expecting the president to check up on us regularly, so I want to ensure you are as comfortable and safe as I can make you," Rozakov said.

Now Rozakov's actions made sense. "Thank you. I'll tell the president of your care." Zamira knew how this was going to work. If she complimented her care to the president, then Bek might find Rozakov useful in the future for other tasks. In a country where furthering career and gaining wealth was based on influence and corruption, Rozakov could use any influence that even a special prisoner may get her.

"You have a room to yourself in here."

Rozakov showed her into a tiny room that contained a bed and a metal sink. A small window the size of two bricks higher up the wall let in a little light. The only other illumination was from a dim ceiling bulb almost buried into the concrete above.

"If you go to the main hall in a few minutes, you'll be able to get some food."

Rozakov turned smartly and left Zamira in her matchbox-sized room, alone for the first time since she'd returned to Tarinor. She hadn't expected such preferential treatment. Those female guards were still here, but she had to hope Rozakov would protect her...until she didn't give away her father's whereabouts. No doubt she'd experience the regular treatment of prisoners then.

But that concern was for another day. She was hungry. She hadn't eaten since her breakfast in Paris, and she needed to keep her strength up for whatever was coming. After some food, she'd return to her new, and hopefully temporary, home to take stock, think her way through what was happening, and get some rest.

After she'd found food and been stared at by the whole prison population, guards, inmates, and children, she'd gone back to her room. An older woman with her graying hair in a braid had followed her.

"I'm sorry, auntie, but if you want something from me or you're going to tell me I need to follow some unknown rules, then you're out of luck. I'm exhausted. I need a toilet and then I need some sleep," Zamira said. Auntie was a term used in Tarinor to address older women with respect even if they weren't family. She hoped that by using it, she would take any rudeness away from being distant and unfriendly. She prepared to defend herself, in case.

The woman laughed. "You certainly have spirit. I'll give you that." She walked into Zamira's cell, sat on the end of her bed, and patted the spot beside her. "I'm Kamilla. I met your father a few years ago when he was starting out his fight against the government, and he helped me. Not that it did much good, because the government still managed to put me in here. But I can help you."

Zamira sat next to her and breathed out in relief. "Thank you, Kamilla. I'm worn out and overwhelmed." She put her hands in her lap and hoped that Kamilla wouldn't be too kind otherwise she'd melt into tears.

"The toilets and showers are together in one room down there," Kamilla said, gesturing down the corridor to the left. "I'll show you in a moment. But you must never go in there on your own. You understand? Never. I have a group of friends who'll also help you. Always take one of us with you. You'll get to meet them all tomorrow, but I think you're too tired for now. In the future, if you need to sleep earlier than the cell doors are locked, tell me, and one of us will keep an eye on you." She looked out the cell door and blew out a long breath. "It's not safe."

Zamira shook her head. She'd been frightened enough since coming to Tarinor. "Violent women in here was one of my worries when I realized where I was," she said.

"There aren't many," Kamilla said. "It's the guards. You're fresh meat, and some of them will be after you. After lockdown is always difficult. Although they can't open a cell until there are two female guards present, there is often trouble." She clenched her jaw. "I expect you've already met some of them."

"Yes. The Russian woman scared the life out of me when I came in. She was about to give me a cavity search with an audience of two other guards, but Rozakov came in and spared me that indignity." Zamira closed her eyes against the all-too-fresh memory.

"Some of the guards are all right. I'll point them out over the next few days. Some are difficult, and some are dangerous. Daytime is much easier to stay safe." Kamilla stood. "I'll take you to the toilet now and when you come back, you go to bed. You shut your door, and I'll keep my eyes on the corridor until lockdown. Tomorrow is another day."

Zamira was almost tearful with exhaustion as she went with Kamilla and followed her instructions about getting into bed and closing her door. She lay in bed. Her emotions bubbled close to the surface, ready to explode. Her thoughts twisted and twirled as if she were on a roller coaster. She drifted from concerns about her father and what he would do to help her, to her future and how her life might change because of this. How long would she be stuck here? Forever? Or would they execute her when she didn't give them the information they wanted, the information she didn't have? She knew her father loved her, but she'd never been able to control her anger at him for following a path that had endangered the whole family. She didn't want to believe that the greater good could beat the desire to keep one's family safe.

The following morning, a klaxon woke her, and she washed and dressed. Her cell door opened, and she stuck her head around the door. Kamilla and a couple of other women appeared.

"Quick. Time for food," Kamilla said.

Zamira joined them, and they walked to the hall as a group and stood waiting for food.

"This is Fariza, and this is Gulia. They are my friends, and now they are your friends. They will help keep an eye on you. If you need help, we are the people to talk to," Kamilla said.

The women ahead of her in the queue had stopped staring at her this morning. She wasn't such a show object as she had been the previous evening. Zamira looked around. This wasn't fine dining. Even her university student restaurant beat it hands down. The central hall served as a general leisure area in the daytime, and the foldaway chairs and tables were pulled out for meals at the kitchen end, so it had a temporary air about it. The windows, some in the walls and some in the roof, were barred and provided filtered light but made the room a little dark. They queued up to a metal counter that held their food. When she got there, Zamira was served the traditional Tarin breakfast of flatbread with either sausage or jam by a couple of fellow prisoners.

Once they had their food and green tea, they found a table to sit at with other women already seated and eating. A female guard appeared in front of Zamira. She wasn't much older than Zamira but much taller and physically well-built. She spoke Tarin as a native. Zamira said nothing, as she had been instructed the day before.

"When you've finished your food, you are to report to Sarai for work today. This will be your job until further notice."

Zamira nodded. The guard went back to her post, leaned against the far wall, and stared at her. Zamira shook her head, as if that might shake away the woman's stares and continued eating her meal.

"That's Neelab," Kamilla said. "She's one of the guards you need to be careful with."

"She's frightening," Zamira said. "I'm lucky I have protection because of the media attention, if it lasts. The day I'm paraded in front of the cameras and there is something wrong, I hope there will be an outcry."

Kamilla shrugged. "Neelab will wait for a chance. She won't do anything where there is a witness. Never be alone, and you will not give her a chance."

Throughout the day, Neelab continued to brazenly glare at her. Zamira did her best to ignore her, but there was something disquieting about her wide-eyed stare. Kamilla told her to ignore her. She found that a lot easier once she'd been allocated duties. She was put with Fariza and Gulia, Kamilla's friends, and set to sewing women's clothes which the prison sold to make money. She had no sewing skills at all despite her mumma hoping she'd inherited some of her needlework expertise. That had led to a number of conversations between her teachers and her mother about the abilities and gifts a woman needs to attract a man. She'd always tuned out.

Having made a number of big mistakes while trying to sew on some buttons, Sarai, the prisoner in charge of the dressmaking, accompanied her to the kitchen and held her out like a specimen in front of the cook.

"Huma," the supervisor said. "Please rescue me. This woman can't sew, but maybe she can chop and stir."

"I'll try her out but if she's no good, you get her back. Agreed?"

"Agreed."

And with that she was gone, and Zamira was left to the cook.

"We make big quantities of food, so I need people like you to chop vegetables and meat and to stir large pans of food. Ever done anything like it before?"

Zamira shook her head. "I'll try hard though. Anything so I don't have to sew."

"This way then. We have carrots and potatoes to work on."

Zamira worked all morning in the kitchen and was happy to be busy. The work wasn't difficult, and the women in the kitchen often sang as they cooked. It was soon lunchtime. Once the meal was over, they cleaned the kitchen, and Zamira had some free time. She sat in a quiet spot in the hall and let the noise and bustle flow around her. Kamilla gave her a book on the history of Tarinor, but although she had it open, Zamira didn't really take in any of the words. She was enjoying being completely mindless.

Soon enough it was suppertime, and she had more kitchen duties making soup. Once again, they cleaned the kitchen down, and Zamira was given an apple—a perk of being kitchen staff. She sat in the hall with Kamilla and shared her apple with her as most of the women watched TV.

After the cell doors locked that night, Zamira was restless. In her mind, Neelab's gray eyes followed her around her cell. She couldn't lose them. Her stomach clenched as she tried to get a handle on her thoughts.

The overhead light buried in the ceiling began flashing, and a klaxon sounded. She jumped out of bed. Would this be one of the nighttime visits Kamilla had warned her about? Gulov had said she would be protected and so had Rozakov. But what did that protection mean in the middle of the night when neither of them were there? She turned to her sink and vomited. She was busy running water into the sink when her cell door opened.

"Stand still with your hands out in front of you," Neelab said. "Madina and I will search your cell for contraband."

The person behind Neelab came into view. It was the wolverine woman from the counter.

"You don't know how lucky you are, Zamira Saliev. You were saved yesterday. If you didn't have all these people looking out for you, we would've been on that bed tonight. Neelab likes to watch before enjoying herself too. Works for me."

Madina walked around her, close but not touching. Zamira tried to control her dizziness, and her legs went weak. She wondered if she could manage to last. She held her breath.

"Your protection will run out one day, and we'll be here. You'll be mine, and I will take you as often as I like. I'm looking forward to your father not claiming you," Madina said and licked her lips.

Zamira desperately tried to control her bladder. It seemed as if she'd been standing here for an hour. Although logic told her it wasn't the case.

"If you weren't frightened and worried before, you should be now. Kapitan Gulov has told us that you are off-limits. But he has also promised that he will let me know the minute that changes."

They left the cell, the door closed, and the automatic lock slammed into the door frame. Zamira remained frozen with her hands out. The bitterness and violence in Madina's voice kept her paralyzed. The darkness in the cell mirrored her feelings. Madina had put a face to her worries. She eventually managed to sit on her bed. She didn't shut her eyes. Somehow, that would let Madina know she was frightened.

The klaxon sounded, and she was still sitting on her bed. The door to her cell automatically opened, and Kamilla and her friends stood there.

"We thought it was you in the night. She usually waits a few more nights. There's nothing we can do but pick up the pieces then. Are you hurt?"

Zamira opened her mouth to speak, but no words seemed to come out. She shook her head and that brought her out of her stupor. "Nothing happened. She frightened me. No, that's too simple. She scared me so much that I sat here all night, too frightened to move. And she promised that she would visit as soon as my protection was revoked." Tears streamed down her face, but she couldn't make a sound. She didn't need sympathy. That would destroy what small confidence she had left.

Kamilla must have understood. "Come on, let's get food and make this a good day. There are meals you need to be preparing in the kitchen," she said.

Later, Zamira scrubbed dirty pans. Despite everything, she'd been lucky so far, but now her life was here with Madina and Neelab. The thought made her skin crawl. There was a warm presence close behind her, and she turned to look into Neelab's cold eyes.

"Come with me," she said.

This was the moment something was going to happen. She paid little attention to where she was going. Her awareness came back as she was standing at the door of Madame Rozakov's office. She was ushered in. She went from concrete flooring to thick carpet, bare walls to flock wallpaper, and metal furniture to dark walnut wood. Madame sat behind her desk with a brown folder in front of her. Neelab shoved her over to the desk and indicated she stand in front of it before she turned and left the room.

"Saliev, we need to talk," Madame said. "Kapitan Gulov will be here in a few minutes. I hope that you will give me a good recommendation as to your treatment. I will then continue to keep your welfare in mind."

Zamira was mesmerized by her thick mascara, eyeliner, and orange lipstick. "Yes, madame. I have been well treated," Zamira said, "and will tell the kapitan so if he asks me."

"Good. I think you look well enough, and I see you have your own clothes back. I believe the kapitan is coming to brief you for another press conference in the morning."

The door opened behind her, letting in a blast of cold, disinfected air and the faint sounds of women's voices. The distinctive smell of Gulov's aftershave preceded him on the cool breeze.

"Madame Rozakov, it's good to see you," Gulov said. "Miss Saliev, I hope our protection is still working. I need to know where your father is. His time is running out for coming and getting you, and therefore, so is yours." He moved so that he was standing at the side of the desk. Madame moved to stand next to him.

"I don't know where my father is. As I told you before, I haven't seen him since I left Tarinor two years ago," Zamira said. "I can't tell you what I don't know."

Gulov handed her a piece of folded paper. "We'll work on your statement for tomorrow. Look this over, it's what you'll be reading to the media." He leaned forward and took Zamira's jaw in his right hand. "The president is losing patience, and that means you'll need to get your father here quickly." He let go of her. "We'll get him here soon or your life will be extremely unpleasant."

Her knees weakened at the ominous warning, but she refused to show the terror running through her. She had to hold on to the possibility, however slim, that help would come. The alternative was unthinkable.

CHAPTER FOUR

FLICK HAD BEEN WALKING for the best part of a day, and there was probably at least another day's trek ahead. She'd been thinking of the times she'd had such fun with Chalky, Slim, and Leah. Holidays in the Spanish sunshine were a highlight. They would all meet up and have fun for a few days, then Chalky and Slim would leave, and she and Leah would spend time in each other's arms.

She hurt. Sure, it was a physical thing after the crash, and her balance was off, so she'd spent most of the day lurching across the plain. She could hardly breathe and fought against the nausea. But the worst hurt was inside. Her stumbling reflected her mind. She'd worked hard at focusing on the good times they'd all had, but in the end, it came back to the fact that she was bearing this burden alone. Her anger thrummed through her. She was the one left to bear this anguish; her love and her friends had been taken too early. She couldn't let Chalky, Slim, and Fitz's sacrifice be worthless; she had to be successful. She tensed and forced herself to keep moving.

She took in a deep breath of dry desert air. She'd decided she shouldn't be sitting in an office in London every day and that she should be in the field, that she should let go of her old life and start to move forward. But when she'd tried to do that, she lost her best friends. What the hell was the answer? Where was she supposed to be?

As the sun began to set, she found a spot behind some rocks to spend the night. She took stock of what she had and where she was. She had money and a burner phone. She had a small amount of food, a petrol stove, small pan, and water bottles. She had a couple of weapons and ammunition.

Would news of the downed helo filter its way to intelligence in Tarinor? And would they think that someone was trying to rescue Zamira? It was a possibility, but hopefully the tribesmen would think that the people onboard were all dead and that no one had walked away. She was a professional, and she'd left no tracks. Her current worry revolved around getting into the prison on her own.

The weakest part of the plan was driving from Tarinor to the border. There was only one road, and she'd hoped that the explosives and sniper expertise of the team would help them get out. She'd looked at two routes across the mountains in case the road was a no-go. But the rugged, harsh terrain wasn't conducive to a rescue. The effort on Flick's trained body would be a push, but it would be brutal for Zamira. The higher route would only be good to use in an emergency, and Flick prayed she wouldn't need it.

Closing her eyes, she began to create a mental map of her strategy. She would go to Sayeb and get a look at the town, the prison, and the layout. She would need to find a cheap and reliable car in Sayeb. After thinking through the possibilities, she gripped her weapon tightly, put her back to the rock, and slept.

A noise woke her. Her old skills hadn't deserted her. She opened her eyes; her hand was still on her weapon. She didn't move a muscle. She waited as the noise got closer. Someone was coming toward her, and given the sound of falling stones, they weren't being careful. Hopefully it was a goat, hungry and looking for food. A grunt confirmed it was definitely an animal, and then there was the sound of more steps over the rocks. The band of goats barely glanced at her as they roamed past.

Dawn painted the sky in strands of pale pink and orange. She drank some water and grimaced. She was already missing her strong double espressos and would kill for a sticky breakfast pastry. She made do with a protein bar, rose, and stretched out her limbs. Sleeping on the rocks didn't get any easier, and the blanket that she carried over her shoulder hadn't kept her warm.

She set out at a fast pace, needing to cover a good distance. The sooner she found her target, got her out, and headed home, the better.

***

It was early afternoon when she saw Sayeb spread out in the valley below her. The river had widened as she walked along the path, and there had been no way to cross for many miles. If she followed this route, she could see she would eventually come to a cinder road that went over a bridge into the town. The town was set in a Y shape as two rivers met, and the prison nestled at the far end between two mountains in the distance. It was a large concrete-block building with several wings and small, dark windows. It had high walls and wire-net fencing. There was a small housing area beside it, with a basic fence surrounding the somewhat dilapidated-looking houses. Children played in the dusty space around them.

The town of Sayeb bustled. There were a number of young people in the streets heading away from a set of red-roofed, white buildings at the other end of the valley from the prison, and she assumed they were probably from the university and had finished classes for the day. The ability to blend into a crowd was exactly what she needed.

She identified a secluded beach area on the bank of the river below her and went down to get herself clean. She removed most of her clothes and washed quickly in the icy cold water. She dried herself off on her blanket. Showing up stinking and filthy would set her apart, and she needed to be as unnoticeable as possible.

As she moved down to the town she started running through her mental checklist of what needed doing. Time was the most important thing. A room, clothes, food, car, meet with contact. Figure out how to get into and out of the prison and away from the people who would most certainly be pursuing them. Easy enough.

She found a shop selling T-shirts and bought a pink glittering shirt proclaiming New York on the front that would be slightly too small for her. There were a number of places offering rooms, mostly hostels, but she couldn't share with men as she needed to lose her tribesman clothing for the next phase of her operation. Flick came across a busy hostel with a number of students of both sexes going in and out. This would suit her purpose. She booked a room for two nights and went upstairs.

The room was small and slightly grubby, with worn, shiny carpet and peeling wallpaper, but the bedding looked clean. The water use was controlled across the whole of Tarinor, so cleaning seemed to be one of those things that wasn't done often. Bigger places could sometimes get premium access, but this wasn't one of them.

Next on her mental checklist was clothing. Her disguise as a tribesman would be good for the rescue, but she had to get into the hotel and meet her contact, and to do that, she had to pass as a woman. She removed her upper body clothes and the band from around her breasts that had flattened what little feminine shape she had and then put on the skimpy T-shirt. She hid one canvas shoulder bag with all her kit in it under the bed. Behind the headboard, the wiring for the room was exposed, and the wall around it had started to crumble. Flick wrapped her two pistols in her bag and jammed it into the hole around the exposed wiring.

She left her room to get something a bit dressier that would highlight her foreignness, but she was counting on that to ensure she didn't look out of place in the Hotel Atlas in Sayeb. One of the shops selling Western clothes for the students had a whole section of fashions, and Flick found what she needed, including a cheap pair of shoes. She spoke as little and as softly as possible. She implied she was a post-doc student at the university and wanted something a little special. The clerk barely glanced at her, which was perfect.

At the hostel, she changed into her new purchases and put some cash in her pocket. She headed into the center of town for some food and to meet up with her contact in the Hotel Atlas. On a mission, Flick either wasn't hungry at all or she could eat for two. There appeared to be no rhyme or reason. But today she was hungry and wondered what a Tarinor international hotel would serve in the way of food. The ubiquitous lamb or goat, she suspected.

The hotel was just like hundreds of hotels around the world with lots of glass, steel, and tiled floors. The restaurant was much busier than she expected, and there were people of all nationalities around the tables. She ordered her lamb and bread in Russian and ate quietly, trying unsuccessfully to hear the conversation around her. Flick always struggled to eat a meal when she was on her own. She'd never gotten used to her feeling that other people thought she wasn't worthy of friends, or that she wasn't good enough for company. She tended to brazen it out and return any stares with a look of bored disdain. The thought that she should have been eating this meal with her team, with her friends, made the food nearly come back up. Her eyes watered, and she blinked hard. Time to hit the bar.

Her shoes sank into deep red carpet, and the air was thick with cigarette smoke despite some open windows. The sound of conversation was loud and almost created a physical barrier to entering the bar, which was also packed with foreigners. There was a real mix of languages from

American and Spanish to French and Japanese.

Flick went to the counter. "What's happening here?" she asked the bartender in Russian.

"It's that girl that was kidnapped. They'll be showing her off tomorrow, trying to get her father to take her place. The whole world's media is here making sure they get coverage that's better than anyone else's," he said. "Vultures."

Would the media frenzy make this easier or harder? Cameras everywhere wasn't generally a good thing. *Fuck.* "I'll take a Sayeb beer, please."

Flick found an ideal seat at the end of the bar and nursed her drink as she watched the people around her. She didn't let her gaze linger on any one person. All she could do was wait and hope her contact would approach.

Sitting farther along the bar were a couple of French guys drinking shorts and discussing the results of a rugby match against Ireland. Flick guessed at scotch or brandy. Behind her was a group of British reporters laughing and joking with each other about some party in London they'd been to. Would her contact approach with all these people around? If anything, they'd blend in and just be two women having drinks. It looked worse that she was drinking alone, but there wasn't anything she could do about that.

A woman sat next to her. She was attractive, with short dark hair and dangling gold earrings shaped as small birds, and her Chanel N°5 perfume pervaded the air around them. Flick nodded and spoke to the barman in Tarin. She could speak and understand Tarin, but it wasn't her strongest language, so she only used it in an emergency.

"Beer, please," the woman said.

"The local beer is good. I hadn't expected it," Flick said in Russian.

"We like to surprise people in Sayeb. Are you visiting with the press?" the woman asked.

"I'm here because an old friend asked me to come and visit his family. But it's difficult to do with the current restrictions," Flick said. "I'm Kia, by the way." She turned to the woman and smiled.

The woman smiled back, and her earrings bobbed like kites in the wind. "Hello. I'm Lily."

"I think you may be able to help me," Flick said. "Can I buy red socks in Sayeb?"

"You may, depending on if you need more than six pairs," Lily said.

Flick nodded. Passwords were good—red socks and six. Step one. "I'd like my friend's relative to come home with me. To do that, I'd need to pick them up and take them away. I don't know if or how that might be possible," Flick said.

"It's certainly possible, although not easy. And it's risky." Lily sipped her drink and glanced casually around the room.

"I understand. Where can we go to talk about the possibilities?" Flick asked.

Lily frowned ever so slightly. "This is the best place possible. I'm in here most nights when I'm not working. I often talk to visitors, so tonight is no different. Perhaps we can move away from the bar when we spot a free table. You can buy me another beer."

Flick tilted her head in acknowledgement and motioned toward a table that had just been vacated. Lily sauntered over, smiling at a few people and saying hello. She really was a regular. They chatted about the recent films released in Tarinor that were a little behind the rest of the world.

"I've spent a lot of time watching films about Europe and the US and dreaming about how to get myself there. I save and save my money. One day I'll make it," Lily said. "And in the meantime, I think I can help you. It'll be expensive. It isn't going to be easy to fix this. Your friend's relative is of high value." She motioned subtly to the room packed full of reporters.

Flick expected this. The bargaining for Zamira Saliev was always going to be hard, and it would be expensive to get her out of prison. It would have been easier to break into a hideaway where she and her team could have used force and their expertise. The cost, which originally was in terms of money, weapons, and explosives, now included three lives. "I understand your position. What do you have in mind? Can you make this happen quickly?" Flick asked.

Lily ran her finger around her beer glass and didn't make eye contact. "Five thousand US dollars, and it can happen tomorrow," Lily said.

In her dreams. "Tomorrow is good, but we have a counteroffer. I've been authorized to offer you help with a visa to Europe and a job once you get there. It means no money will change hands. If this job is successful, a one-way ticket will be added."

There was silence. Lily's eyes were wide as she seemed to search

Flick's face for any hint of a lie. "I hadn't expected that offer. I thought we'd bargain over money," she said.

"Our mutual friend thought that if you helped him with his problem that you should be repaid the best he could offer," Flick said.

"Yes." Lily slowly nodded. "I get it. No need to bargain. I accept. I've planned the escape already. Doing something tomorrow around the press conference would be too difficult, and security will expect that a rescue may be attempted then. It'll be tomorrow evening, and you'll need to pick her up from the prison."

"Right. How will this happen?" *Fucking hell.* Flick hated being so dependent on someone else's planning.

"She'll escape from the kitchen back door. There's a caged area around the rubbish bins, and there are kitchen staff, prisoners, and guards going in and out all day. The guards smoke there too. The kitchen door will not be locked because a number of us will be using it. The cage is double-strand wire netting. I'll ensure that a hole is cut in the netting tonight behind the biggest bin for the relative to crawl out of. From there..."

She shrugged, clearly trying to look blasé. Her tense jaw and the way her fingernails drummed a staccato dance on the table suggested otherwise. It wasn't reassuring. "I take it I can get a car close enough?" Flick asked.

"No. You'll be parked in the wide pull-in on the dirt road nearby. Your relative will come to you."

Flick worked a napkin between her fingers, tearing it to tiny shreds. "She'll be out in the open. Exposed."

Lily didn't look concerned. "You'll need to leave immediately. The relative will be missed quite quickly after getting out. She is noticeable, and several of the guards have their sights set on her," Lily said.

The thought made Flick wince. No details of that part were necessary.

"The most important thing though: how do I know that your offer will happen? I was always told as a child that if an offer is too good to be true, then it is. I'm not sure I want to take this amount of risk for a promise," Lily said.

"Yes, but what a promise. You know who we're talking about, and you have a contact who will give you the full details. Tell them I'm here and alive, and it *will* happen. You have my word if you're inclined to believe me."

Lily nodded. "I am sure our mutual friend will come through."

Flick hoped that she'd been convincing enough as she left the bar and returned to her hostel room. She needed to get some sleep but was still too wired. She sat fully clothed on her small hard bed and tried to get some order to her thoughts.

But that led her down a dark path as she replayed the crash. The bruises on her chest, abdomen and legs mimicked the colors of the explosion. The sudden ache in her stomach and the rush of air from her lungs added to the feeling of being sucked into a void. Slim and Chalky were gone. The tears ran down her cheeks, and she didn't stop them. It would be a long while before she could look at a hot chocolate without thinking of them both. Their loss hit hard, and she eventually cried herself to sleep.

The morning brought with it an emotional headache. The magnitude of what she was doing hit her. She lay on her bed and listened to the everyday noises surrounding her, of people getting on with their day, and she allowed the pain of loneliness to circle her for a minute. She swallowed it down. It was no good feeling sorry for herself. She was on her own for now. HQ would know of the crash but had probably assumed they were all dead. She didn't think they'd mount another op. It had been difficult enough to finance this one. Hopefully Lily would talk to her contact and get the message through that she was alive.

The escape was possible, and she could do it. A good soldier always stayed on task, and she didn't have the luxury of thinking about what ifs. She rose and started into her day, ready for the challenge she knew was coming.

She left the hostel dressed as a tribesman. She had to find a vehicle, look at her escape route from the prison, and work out the direction she should take. She needed to sort a car first. Once she had one, she could use it as a base and spend the day out of sight of people. The local car market was on a small patch of dirt with a wooden hut at the back. Most cars in Tarinor were held together with lots of repairs, and she needed something that would get her out of the country over mountain roads. She looked around the dozen or so cars in the lot, and the salesman came toward her. He wore the ubiquitous Tarin sunglasses and a suit two sizes too small to cover his rounded belly. His cheap aftershave barely covered the underlying sour smell of sweat.

"Show me the engine on this one," Flick said, not allowing any greeting or chit chat. She was going to be all business. The salesman unlocked the car from a bunch of keys from around his neck and lifted the hood. Flick had a little knowledge of mechanics from her father's farm and could see the engine was well cared for. She nodded, climbed into the car, and started the engine. It would do. "I have three hundred," Flick said.

The man sucked his teeth. "I want seven."

And so started their dance. Flick left the mart once, and the man returned to his shack as if not caring. In the end, Flick paid four hundred Tarin dollars and knew she had a bargain. She found a space in a row of parked cars in the center of Sayeb not far from the street market. She opened the window and leaned against it. She could smell the lack of water everywhere. Everything stank of sewage, and drains, and sweat. She figured they didn't notice it after a while but Flick still did. She opened the passenger window and hoped for a breeze to let the air through. There were several people in the street going to and from the market, and she was pleased to be somewhere she was unlikely to be noticed.

The market was typical of the area: a lot of small stalls with fresh produce alongside shops with open fronts. The wind direction changed, and the air held the fresh smell of fruit and vegetables. She went through her bags to look at what she needed and what she could buy that would be useful on their outbound journey. She left the quiet of her car for the noise and bustle of the market. The women wore a mix of Western dresses and traditional, colorful Tarin trousers and overdresses. The men were typically in a mixture too, although most were in shades of brown. The noticeable contrast was between traditional toki headware and baseball caps. She shopped for some snack bars and water bottles, which were expensive, but the bottles would be useful. There was little here to buy that would be good as food for their journey as it was all fresh and unlikely to last more than a day. She bought some flatbreads, sausage, sour cream, butter, and a melon. She stored it all in the back of the car and sat back in the front, eating an apple.

She had to figure out how she was going to get Zamira Saliev out of the country. Her previous plan had them driving out along the main mountain road at speed, using Slim and Chalky's firepower to help them on their way. She left the town and followed the route for several miles and decided it was the best option. It was certainly the fastest and least dangerous. She needed a plan B if the road proved too treacherous, or if they were chased, and she didn't have enough firepower. They'd have to go over the high plains in an emergency. Flick thought her way through the maps in her head and decided where they could leave the road. She drove to that point, and it was as she'd hoped. The climb would be stiff until they were on the plains and crossing them would be hard before coming down to a checkpoint and out. It would be a difficult trek this time of year, but the mountain routes were still snow-covered, and they probably wouldn't survive the cold. In the event of something happening closer to Sayeb, she had a plan C which she didn't want to use at all. Almaz Saliev had mentioned that Zamira knew of a Lyulli village close by that may help. Flick didn't want to rely on help from strangers, especially so close to Sayeb.

She changed her top and shoes and removed her headdress while she was out in the mountains, returned to the town as a Westerner, and parked in the hotel carpark. She entered the reception to see if she could get into the government's media show. There was also a chance that she might be able to rescue Zamira here and not use the prison. As she entered the front door, she noted armed guards on most of the service doors. Maybe she'd have managed with the rest of the team, but a solo op was out of the question. Accreditation cards were being checked, and Flick decided it was probably best to watch it on the TV in the bar. As she went into the bar, a group of British journalists passed her, and Flick saw an opportunity.

"Are you going to see Zamira Saliev?" she asked.

A bearded man turned and carried on walking slowly. "Yes. Should be interesting to see what story the government comes up with. We missed the first press conference."

"I missed that media show too. I think it was too soon after the event. I'm waiting for the government story," Flick said as they walked past the accreditation desk and went into the room. She moved along with them and sat next to the bearded man. A few minutes later she caught her first glimpse of Zamira Saliev, a small, dark-haired woman with her hair pulled back. She looked very pale, which her dark eyes accentuated. Flick knew the security was too tight to rescue her now. She would have to take a chance on Lily and plan for escape this evening. She hoped that she was in time and that nothing untoward happened to Zamira before then.

CHAPTER FIVE

IT WAS ANOTHER DAY in the prison, and Zamira gave her thanks that she'd had another night without being disturbed. She didn't know what she thought about the forthcoming press conference. Half of her wanted to make sure that her father didn't give in to the president. The government was a corrupt institution the people of Tarinor didn't deserve. Zamira still raged at the thought of her mumma being murdered and didn't want to give Tarinor any more Saliev blood, either hers or her father's.

Kamilla and her friends picked her up on their way to the morning meal, and Zamira diverted as she began her duties in the kitchen to prepare the midday meal. She enjoyed the kitchen first thing in the morning. There was reflected light from the windows in the roof, and the air was still clear and not yet full of steam and the smell of cooking food. It was a moment of solitude in the dark chaos her life had become. As the day progressed, she was once again on lunchtime duty and had finished preparing the usual lamb and vegetables when she was brought out of her thoughts by the sound of a door opening. A guard was passing through for a smoke, probably. But it was Neelab to collect her and take her to Madame's office. It was press conference time.

Kapitan Gulov waited in the corridor for her along with Madame Rozakov and two of the female guards from the prison. They were all armed. The guards came to stand on either side of her, and she was handcuffed to one of them. They moved out of the building and into a black car waiting in the prison yard. Any hope of rescue while she was beyond the prison walls was dashed.

The car headed into town and stopped at the Hotel Atlas. Zamira remembered it from her days here as a student, although she had rarely been inside it. It catered for foreigners who had the money to pay their high prices. There were a number of town police standing outside the hotel's rear entrance keeping a distant group of photographers back. Their car stopped and Zamira was bundled out. She tried to look at the cameras, but the guards pushed and pulled her through the corridor of policemen into the hotel. She didn't notice much along the way except a painted red concrete floor and the smell of polish. It became noisy with the sound of loud voices and banging metal pans or trays. They went up some stairs, and she was in a different place. Carpet was soft beneath her feet, and the quiet buzz of conversation filtered through her simmering panic. She could smell coffee, and her taste buds reacted. Her eyes filled with tears at the mundane desire for something so simple.

They entered a small anteroom, and her handcuffs were removed.

Kapitan Gulov handed her the written statement. "Refresh yourself about this," he said. "As we discussed, you will not deviate from the words. You will not answer any questions. Is that clear?"

"Yes," Zamira said. Her hands trembled as she read the paper, the words blurring through her tears. Before she had time to think, she was standing in front of a large room full of people with TV cameras with large lenses on the front and sound equipment situated everywhere. This was ten times bigger than her last press conference, and she could tell by the insignias, it included a lot of international stations. There was silence in the room. She could hear the sound of china cups clattering somewhere and then a door closed, and it was completely quiet.

She tried to smile at the cameras and read her short statement. It was difficult to do when her hands were shaking so much, but she managed it. Once she had finished, the silence continued for a moment. "Papa, I love you," she said. She turned and was led back into the anteroom and back to the prison the way she had come. Within minutes, she was back in the kitchen preparing food as if she had never been away. No sense of rescue, no possibility of someone who cared whether or not she lived or died here. And Neelab's salacious grin made it so much worse.

Later that day, the kitchen was hot and full of steam, but somehow Zamira could breathe here. The women needed feeding and while she was working here, no one bothered her. She followed instructions from the head cook, who was employed by the prison. All of her staff were prisoners, and there was a relaxed atmosphere. The prisoners sang as they did menial tasks that didn't require any concentration, and Zamira found herself joining in despite not wishing to get used to being in the prison.

The kitchen suddenly became silent, and the air became supercharged.

A guard must have entered. The guards often snuck out the back to have a cigarette amongst the trash cans. Zamira continued to stir the soup she'd been making and kept her head down. If she wasn't noticed then she hoped there'd be no comments about her living in the West and all her money, how they could do things to her body if they were given a chance, the things they whispered as she walked past or said outright as they passed her cell. The back door opened, there was a blast of cold air, and it was if the kitchen collectively breathed out.

A few minutes later, there was a rattling of keys. The door opened and closed. She continued stirring in the silence of expectation. She noticed the smell of cigarette smoke, and the hairs on the back of her neck all rose as she became conscious of a guard standing behind her. She calmed her breathing but couldn't stop the panic that seemed to take over her body. She was trying not to run away; her mind had already left, and her body wanted to catch up.

The guard whispered in her ear. "I've just received a wonderful surprise from your father, I assume."

Zamira swallowed. Her father? She kept stirring, waiting.

"Once the meal is over and the kitchen cleaned, the back door will be unlocked. Duck behind the biggest trash can and go out through the hole in the cage. Walk out toward the big boulder, and someone will be there to meet you. Don't mess this up, and we'll both get what we want," the guard said before she turned and left.

This was unreal. It could be a plan to get her to try and escape so that the guards could get her where they wanted her. She didn't have time to think about that possibility in any detail. If it was an escape, she didn't want to miss it. If it was something else, then so be it.

Once the evening meal finished, Zamira volunteered to wash the kitchen floor, knowing she'd be the last person there. She worked her way over to the door and took a deep breath. This was it. The door opened easily and quietly. Her heart was beating so loudly in her head that she wondered if she'd ever hear if there was someone behind her.

She closed the door quickly behind her. It was dark outside, but there was a light above the door. She slid into the shadows, trying not to gag at the smell of rotting food and cigarette smoke. She moved behind the biggest trash can and found a hole in the wire netting, just as the guard had promised. She squeezed through it, snagging her top. She froze as she yanked on it, and it tore. The sound seemed to reverberate like a jet engine in the empty alley. No one came out, so she pushed through and ran.

A figure stood up from behind the rocks. Zamira faltered. She didn't think her heart could beat any faster, nor her breath be any more reedy. She'd just left the world of the prison. Though dangerous, it was relatively safe. She knew what the problems were. Now she was outside, and she had no idea who this person was or what they were going to do. They could take her away and extort money from either the government or her father. Surely staying in the prison was worse... She nearly lost her footing as fear made it hard to keep moving.

The person spoke in Tarin. Zamira didn't have words to reply. So, the man used Pashtun. Finally, they spoke in French, clearly assuming she didn't understand rather than that she was too paralyzed with fear to speak.

"Zamira. Your father sent me. We need to get going."

Zamira still hadn't spoken. She nodded. She got into the car. It was ancient, and the door didn't close properly. It took two attempts to start but once on the road, the car moved along at a good speed, although it sounded more like a truck. They went through the town and crossed the bridge. The road on the other side was typical of the mountain roads, cinder in places, tarmac in places, and potholes and dirt creating a strange patchwork of decay.

Zamira stared at the man as he drove. He was intent on the road, though he continually looked in the rearview mirror. To drive this road in the dark was a nightmare. The headlights hardly lit anything outside the car. She could just make out his features in the shadows. He had high cheekbones and an almost feminine jaw line. If Zamira was into men, she'd almost think he was attractive. He turned to look at her.

"I think we have company," he said. "I expected you'd be missed very quickly, but I'd hoped we'd get farther away."

Zamira looked behind them and was able to see blue flashing lights heading over the bridge. It looked to be two cars. They were moving very quickly, and at the speed they were traveling, they'd catch up with them in a few minutes. There was the sound of shots firing and flashes of light from behind them.

"They aren't close enough to do much damage unless they're lucky," the man said. "But we do need to get off this road somehow. Your father said to say the word Lyulli to you. Does that help us at all?"

Zamira understood why her father had mentioned the Lyulli. She had been at the International University in Sayeb for her degree and knew where the Lyulli village was. "When we get to where the road widens, take the left-hand side and stay on it. It's a slow turn."

The man nodded keeping his hands tight on the steering wheel.

She continued, nerves making her need to fill the silence. "The Lyulli village is out here, and the police won't dare to enter without an invite, but we need to get into the village and get the car hidden before the police get close, so put your foot down."

Zamira clutched her necklace and thought again of her father. He was protecting his daughter even though he was far away. Her rescuer was a little strange, but Zamira was confident in her own abilities, and she didn't need this man to help her. Well, that wasn't strictly true. She hadn't been able to get out of the prison on her own, and the man *was* driving. But if she had to make it on her own from here, she could. Couldn't she?

With the blue lights growing closer, they came upon a set of high wooden gateposts that marked the opening in the fence. There were no gates, and the fence became a wall not far from where they were. "Switch off your lights. Drive in, and as soon as we can see a left or right turn, we'll leave the main road," Zamira said.

The man did as he was told without saying a word, and they moved slowly, with the car bouncing and jerking over the uneven terrain. "Turn just past that open area. Come on, move. We need to get out of sight quickly." Zamira gestured toward the darkness. "Turn right over there and park in that row of cars. Well, what would be a row of cars if they had wheels."

The man stopped the car where Zamira indicated and switched off the engine. There was silence.

"Come. We'll need to find Grandmother," Zamira said.

"Your grandmother?" He shook his head slightly. "They're likely to look for you at a relative's house if she lives this close. Damn." As the man got out of the car, he turned to Zamira. "I have some small weapons and a little food in here. I'll bring everything with me," he said, already in the back of the car. He came out with a second shoulder bag.

"Yes. Good idea. I don't expect we'll be able to take the car anywhere now," Zamira said. Away from the prison, out of the confines of the car, and able to stand on her own, her confidence began to seep back in. She could do this.

"I should introduce myself. I'm Flick Colonna from London. I work for the UK government, and we're helping your father."

As the man spoke his voice became higher, and Zamira suddenly wondered about her earlier thoughts. She stared openly at the man's face.

"And yes, I'm a woman. I thought it fair to tell you. But it will make no difference. I go into the village as a man."

Zamira's anger flared. Sending a woman to rescue her? And one alone, at that. So far this woman had done little except drive her away from the prison. She'd gotten a clapped-out car that had barely survived a chase and seemed to have little idea about how they were going to get away. Zamira pulled herself from her fugue. This thinking wasn't helpful. "We'll be picked up in a moment by armed guards. I'll do the talking."

"Okay," Flick said, her eyebrow twitching slightly.

As they stood there, Zamira was aware of movement in the darkness. The movement became two shapes, which morphed into two men. Zamira couldn't make them out clearly.

"Why shouldn't we shoot you for trespassing on our land?"

The man's voice was gruff, and the smell of cigarettes wafted in the breeze toward her. He had a lighted cigarette sheltered in his free hand and was holding a machine gun with the other.

"Because I'm asking Grandmother for help. She knows my father." Zamira hoped that the men would leave the decision to Grandmother. The Lyulli were nomadic people who traveled all over the mountains between Afghanistan, Pakistan, and Tarinor. Some had settled and most of the compound worked in the town, doing manual labor, buying scrap metal and cars, running all sorts of scams, and begging if they had nothing better to do. They were a clan society and in Tarinor, it was matriarchal. The head grandmother would always remain at home in the daytime with some of the older generation to look after small children who were too young to earn money. The whole society was outside the normal culture of Tarinor, hence the police would never enter the village, and the Lyulli wandered wherever they wanted to go, crossing country borders at will.

The cigarette man gestured to them. "Come with us. We'll see what she says."

He led the way and the other man followed behind Zamira and Flick as they went through a maze of passages between houses that eventually brought them out at an opening with a house set off by itself. He told them to wait and knocked on the door. The door opened and an elderly woman appeared in traditional Tarin clothing, a gray, shapeless long dress, brightly patterned with red emblems worn over her trousers. She wore a red headscarf, although her gray hair wasn't completely covered.

"Grandmother, it looks like this couple escaped from the police and hid in our compound. The woman asked to be brought to you, saying you knew of her father," the big man said.

This was their make-or-break moment. If Grandmother didn't listen to them, they and their car would be put outside the compound, and they'd be left to fend for themselves. How frightened she'd been over the last week had left its mark, and Zamira felt a rising tide of nausea. These life-or-death moments kept coming, each one more horrendous than the one before.

Grandmother approached them and despite Flick being a foot taller, she commanded the air between them.

"Who are you, that you presume to know me?" Grandmother asked.

Flick didn't move a muscle. She simply looked at the old woman impassively.

"Grandmother, my name is Zamira Saliev, and I don't know you. But my father is Almaz Saliev, and he's in exile. He sent us here for help. He has always had strong links with the Lyulli, and I know he's done a lot to help you. I wear this necklace and bracelet, which were given to him by the grandmother in Denebe, with her thanks." Zamira held up the necklace, which reflected in the dim light around them.

The grandmother looked into her eyes before looking at the necklace and bracelet. "I know of your father. We've always been in debt to him for clearing us from drug traffic charges. We may not be exactly within the law, but we do not traffic drugs, however profitable it may be," Grandmother said. "My son heard about your situation yesterday on TV and told me about it. I saw you myself on TV today. I did not expect to see you tonight."

"My father is causing a lot of problems. The government wants to silence him, and this is their way of doing it. We had to leave Tarinor after they murdered my mother. It wasn't safe for us to stay." Zamira pointed at Flick. "Firuz helped me escape from the prison, but the police are already after us, as your men saw. Can you help us, please?" She waited in the silence as the grandmother studied them. If she turned them away, they were as good as dead.

"I think you'd better come in. Firuz, you too. We'll feed you, and we can talk about what you need. It would be best you leave as soon as possible under cover of darkness so that you'll be well away from the area by the morning. We don't need any more problems with the president here."

Grandmother led them into a room that was obviously a meeting place and had a number of men sitting in it. A room leading from it had a number of women sitting and reclining on the floor. The rooms were lit by two oil lamps giving out a dirty light, and they smelled of sweat, men's cheap aftershave, and cooked lamb. The underlying smell was of sewage and dampness caused by the way the compound had been constructed. None of that mattered. Right now, it was a sanctuary.

Grandmother led them into the back of the building to a small alcove and showed them the remains of the Lyulli meal of lamb and bread. "Zamira. Sort some food for you both. I suggest you stay here and eat."

She took hold of Zamira's hands and looked her up and down. It was disconcerting, and Zamira had to work to keep from pulling away.

"I'm going to find you some different clothes. Your Western clothes are not going to help you. You'll need something warm. Where are you going?"

"Pakistan," Flick said. "I think she will need to be a young boy. It will keep her warmer and from a distance or from the air, we'll look like two goatherds."

"Yes, you'll need warm clothing, boots, and blankets. I'll talk to my granddaughter, and we'll see," Grandmother said and left.

"I'm not certain I want to eat," Zamira said once they were alone. She wasn't certain that the village cooking would help her stomach at all. As a vegetarian, the thick chunks of meat looked disgusting and didn't help her nausea either.

"I'm hungry," Flick said, filling a plate with lamb and grabbing a couple of the local flatbreads. "You should eat. The mountains will be cold, and we have a long journey ahead of us. We won't be able to carry much food either, so we could go hungry toward the end. Enjoy it while you can."

"You may be able to eat, but I'm feeling too sick to be able to swallow anything. My life is on the line here, and I'm worried about how we'll get out." Zamira put her hands on her hips and felt the blood rising to her face. "They sent one person, a woman in a male-dominated society, to help me."

"I'm the person who got you out of prison and the one who's going to get you home. I know where we're going, and when we leave you're going to rely on me. Take your attitude and lose it."

Heat coursed through Zamira's body, and she tensed. This woman had absolutely no idea what she'd been through in the past few days. "Attitude. You think I have an attitude? You're just plain incompetent, getting me out of the prison without a plan. That's amateur at best and deadly at worst," she said.

Flick set down her plate and glared at her. "We had a plan when we left London. There were three of us when we set out, and I'm the only one left. I lost my two best friends and a pilot on our way here. So, if you want to discuss lives on the line, I'm ahead of you." She picked up her plate again.

"You know nothing about being in that prison and the way they treat their women prisoners."

"I know all about that prison and its reputation, along with several others in the countries all around here. The prisons all work on the same idea, that once a woman is a criminal, no one will want her, except as a sex slave. I've rescued several women from the other prisons. You were lucky there, since they didn't have male guards. Other women in prisons with male guards haven't been so lucky."

"Did you have the same trouble rescuing them? Were you just as useless?" By now, Zamira was speaking loudly. She was close to exploding like a firework.

"There's no discussing anything with you, is there?"

The back door opened, and Grandmother came in.

"Come with me," she said to Zamira.

Zamira went out into the dark chilly night and stopped for a moment to get her bearings. Grandmother was ahead of her, and there was light from an open door across her path. The ground appeared to be dusty earth, and the smell of urine and animals was overpowering. Thank goodness she hadn't eaten anything. Zamira hurried to catch up and arrived at the open doorway just as Grandmother entered.

She followed her and was introduced to a young woman who was about the same size and age as Zamira. They pointed to some clothing laid out on the table.

"Put these on and give Golbahar your clothes. She will dispose of them."

Zamira quickly stripped off her T-shirt and jeans and put on the woolen undergarment from the table, followed by a dark brown shirt and matching thick trousers. There was a blanket that wasn't exactly freshly laundered, although Zamira suspected that whatever it smelled of, she wouldn't worry too much when she needed to keep warm. She was given brown turban-like headgear and once her hair was inside it, she realized it would be difficult to tell what sex she was. The biggest surprise was the black leather ankle boots. The leather was soft and worn, but they were comfortable and fit her.

The girl stared open-mouthed at the necklace and bracelet Zamira was wearing. "Did you know these are special to the Lyulli and worth more money than you can imagine?" she asked, putting out a hand to touch the necklace.

"Are they? I had no idea. They're full of memories of my past life and my mother. They were given to my father by the Lyulli as a thank-you. My father gave them to my mother and when my mother died, he gave them to me. I wear them so I feel close to her."

The girl frowned a little and stared at the necklace but looked away at Grandmother's soft reprimand. Something went unsaid, but Zamira decided it would be rude to pry.

Once dressed in the outer clothing, Zamira was considerably warmer. Grandmother handed her an overcoat that would ensure she was well protected against the cold mountain air.

They returned to the kitchen where Flick had just finished her meal and had made herself some green tea. She looked at Zamira and nodded.

"Thank you, Grandmother. The car is where your men picked us up. Please keep it. It's pretty old, but it still runs, and the tires are reasonable. You should get a good price for it." Flick handed Grandmother the keys.

Grandmother took them. "Thank you," she said. "I'll send one of my grandsons with you on the path above us to show you the route into the next valley. By tomorrow you'll be well away from here and in the daylight, the way will be clear to you."

Zamira set off from the compound following a young man dressed almost identically to herself and with Flick behind her. Her head ached, and she still expected her stomach to heave any moment. She needed to survive, and she needed to keep going to do that. Tomorrow was another day.

CHAPTER SIX

FLICK SHIVERED IN THE cold night air. The temperature had fallen throughout the evening and despite walking uphill and exerting herself a little, the icy wind bit through her clothing. She wrapped her blanket more closely around herself. It wasn't easy going, and the man ahead climbed at a speed which showed he knew these mountains well and traversed them often. Zamira walked between him and Flick and had begun to slow down over the last hour.

The man stopped and turned. "We are near the top, perhaps about ten minutes. I'll leave you now, and you should rest until daylight."

Flick looked at Zamira as she sat down heavily on a rock outcrop. She wasn't going to be able to go much farther. She wasn't paying any attention to what was happening, that much was clear. "We'll shelter in these rocks and follow the path at dawn. Thank you for your help in getting us here," Flick said.

"My grandmother says we owe the lady's father a lot, and it's good to be able to repay. Good luck." With that, he disappeared into the darkness.

Flick moved around Zamira and checked the wind direction. They were sheltered from the worst of it by the rocks Zamira was sitting on. Flick found a spot farther around that was ideal for them to lay down and sleep for a few hours.

"We should rest here for a few hours, Zamira." Flick had no acknowledgement that Zamira had heard her. She put her hand on her shoulder. "Come and lie down over here in the shelter of the rocks."

Zamira looked up with glassy eyes. "I'm so tired," she whispered.

Flick picked her up gently under the arms and pulled her upright. Then she led her into the lee of the rocks. She managed to get Zamira to lie down, pulled her blanket over her, and carefully tucked it in. Flick lay down next to her and put her own blanket on top of them both. After their exertion climbing the mountain, Flick was certain that once they settled, they would both feel the cold. "I think we should share body heat, so turn on your side away from me, and I'll pull up close to your back. We'll be warmer and more likely to sleep."

Flick felt Zamira turn away. She wrapped the back of Zamira's body with the front of her own and put an arm over her. Within moments she knew she was warmer. "Goodnight, Zamira," Flick whispered. There was no reply except her heavy breathing. She was already sound asleep. Flick could barely keep her eyes open. Between the rush of the rescue and their long escape, she was exhausted. Part of her wondered if she should try to stay awake and keep watch, but she'd be worthless tomorrow if she was already this tired now. She had to trust they were hidden well enough to avoid detection if anyone happened to be looking in this direction. She closed her eyes, tightened her arm around Zamira, and slept.

She awoke with the sun on her face and a strange, tickling sensation across her lips. Hair. She hadn't had hair in her mouth and across her face since Leah had passed. A chasm appeared in her thoughts as she recalled Leah and all the wonderful times they'd been together. Lying together in the sun in her secluded garden after making love on the grass. They'd fallen asleep, and Flick had woken up with Leah almost lying on top of her. Her long, pretty hair was blowing across Flick's face.

She opened her eyes to find dark hair in her face, and her dream of Leah and her blond hair swiftly disappeared. Her heart ached for the loss of the moment. She was on the side of a mountain in Tarinor with an awkward, disdainful woman who had no idea of the lengths people had gone to rescue her. In her sleep, she looked sweet and relaxed, a far cry from the unimpressed prison escapee. Better to let her sleep for a while.

Flick sat up and searched for her water bottle. Finding good drinking water and food were going to be their biggest problems for the next few days. She had managed to buy a couple of bottles of mineral water, and she'd filled a couple of bottles from the public tap near her hostel and used water purifying tablets. The public taps were only switched on for a few hours a day, so she'd been lucky. Still, in view of the general water quality and risk of disease, it was difficult. They would have to hope for some clear mountain streams and that her supply of water purifying tablets would last them.

Their food was also problematic. She had a small supply of flatbreads, sour cream, and pilaw, a mixture of mutton, rice, and vegetables that was Tarinor's national dish. But it was only good for the first meal. She'd been unable to find anything in Sayeb that would be easy to carry apart from a couple of energy bars. She thought back to how easy carrying army ration packs was. Maybe she could find some rabbits or goats. She had a multifuel burner and a diesel canister that was full, but it might not last more than a few meals. She did the math. One point seven liters of water for every ounce in the canister. She had twenty-eight ounces if she was lucky, so if she heated water for tea and food, they should be good for three or four days.

She needed to stop working out the future and get into the day. She looked down and found Zamira staring at her. She'd been so busy calculating that it was disconcerting to see her awake. "Did you manage to sleep any?" Flick asked.

"Yes, but I kept waking because of the cold," Zamira said.

There wasn't anything to say to that. "I'm just going to run up to the top and have a look at where we are. I'll be back shortly. Can you work a multifuel burner to heat some water?" Flick asked.

"No. But I'm sure if you set it up, I can watch it."

Flick set her small pan on the burner and emptied the remnants of a water bottle into it. "We can have some green tea, and I have some flatbread to eat for breakfast, then we should be on our way." She turned and ran up the path to the top of the mountain pass. She kept close to the ground and looked over. The Lyulli compound was in a small, hidden valley not marked on the maps, which was why she'd temporarily lost her bearings last night. Looking down, she could see the plan B path she'd planned on taking last night. There was a wide valley with sharp sides leading down to the road before they rose again to the low mountain opposite. Flick could also see a mountain stream and waterfall that they would pass later in the day as they traversed the valley. Not only would they have fresh water, but there was no sign of anyone on the road. For now, it was safe.

She returned to Zamira, who barely looked up. "We're where I expected us to be, and we have a hard journey ahead, but we should reach the border with Pakistan in three to four days. We'll avoid any towns or villages unless we need food or water." She checked the water, and it was just boiling. She put green tea into the pan and left it to cool. She took the bread out of her bag, tore a piece in half, and gave half to Zamira.

Zamira looked at it in her hands but remained motionless.

"Are you okay?" Flick asked, biting into her bread.

"Yes, but I'm not sure I can eat anything," Zamira said.

Flick nodded. "I understand. It's hard to eat when your stomach is churning with fear and your mouth is dry. Have some of this tea first. It'll help."

Flick wrapped the corner of her blanket around the tea pan and handed it to Zamira. She started sipping the tea, and Flick breathed easier. If Zamira could drink, then she might eat something afterward. If not, at least she'd be hydrated.

Flick ate her piece of bread and once Zamira had finished drinking, she drank the tea that was left in the pan. "Please try to eat the bread now. We have a long way to go today, and you'll need every ounce of energy you can get."

Zamira picked up the bread and started to eat. "Perhaps I can eat it as we walk," she said.

"Good idea."

They packed up their makeshift camp and put their blankets over their shoulders. Flick picked up both bags and put one across each shoulder. The one by her right hand contained her weapons and ammunition. She wore it to the front, allowing her swift access to the weapon if necessary. "Keep your head down when we get up here. We don't want anyone spotting us if they happen to be looking our way," Flick said.

As they neared the top, they crouched down and carefully peered over. The road they'd turned off last night continued for miles along the valley below. At the moment, it was still empty. "We need to cross over the road and go up the opposite mountain and through the pass over there." Flick pointed to a distinct high valley in the line of mountains in front of them. It was close to the point she'd looked at yesterday for an emergency escape. "If we follow the high valley and cross a high plain at the end of it, we'll end up at the border. I'd like to be at the end of the valley by nightfall."

"Oh, I see where you're going with this," Zamira said. "I know I'm slow. I'll certainly try not to hold you up, *rescuer*. You have to remember, I'm not in the military or an athlete. Leave me behind if you need to. I'll be fine." Her words had sharp, glittering edges.

"I'm not trying to belittle your ability; I was thinking aloud. And while we're chatting," Flick said, trying to ignore the annoyance brought on by

Zamira's tone. "Have you ever used a gun?"

"So now you want me to kill people too? No, I've never shot a gun. I'm a university student, soon to be a doctor. You expect me to run around Paris with my Smith & Wesson, killing bandits on the banks of the Seine? What do you think?" Her eyes widened, and she almost spat the words out.

"I was just curious and, unlike you, I'm not making assumptions. Plenty of people know how to use guns, and you might have been one of them." She closed her eyes and pinched the bridge of her nose, reminding herself to breathe. "But you will need to practice. We'll have a lesson when we have one of our breaks." Losing her temper would achieve nothing.

Zamira, however, was still spinning into a temper tantrum. "You think I'm going to practice shooting? You must be joking. I'm not touching anything that could take a life. You can't force—"

Flick motioned abruptly to show Zamira that she should lose her volume. "Quietly," she whispered. "Unless you want to go back to prison?"

Zamira closed her mouth.

"So, if we're attacked by drug runners and I'm killed, you'll just give up and go and be their plaything? Or if they decide to trade you and auction you off to the highest bidder, you'll just accept that future rather than protect yourself?" Flick asked. "You need to be able to defend yourself if something happens to me."

"I just won't take a life. I'm not made that way," Zamira said. "The life of every living thing is important to me, and I can't imagine any scenario where I'd use a gun in anger."

Flick stood and moved below the horizon. She clenched her fists to not show her anger. It would achieve nothing. She had to make Zamira understand. She'd never been in a situation where she might need to shoot at someone. Surely, she grasped that this was a part of the world where violence was the culture, and drugs, weapons, and sex were the spoils.

"Will you just humor me, please?" Flick's whisper had a sense of desperation to it, but she didn't care. "If you know how to use a gun, I'll be happy. You can decide never to fire it. That's okay. It's your decision. But I'd rather you make the decision knowing how to use one. There would be nothing worse than wanting or needing to use a gun and not knowing how."

Zamira was silent for a long moment. She looked at Flick and scowled. "You make a good argument, and you certainly made your point. Fine, I'll do it, but under protest."

Well, thank fuck for that. She could be reasonable after all. "When we get out of here and you haven't used the gun, you can protest all you want."

Zamira was silent. Flick looked at her closely. She was almost as olive-skinned as Flick, but her complexion was pale, and her hair had that mussed, just slept-in look about it. There were dark shadows under her eyes. Despite that, Zamira was quite beautiful. She'd been lovely to hold in the night despite them both being fully clothed. Flick closed down her thoughts. She was married. No, she was widowed but she still loved Leah, and she wouldn't mess with what they'd had. She shouldn't be thinking these thoughts. She'd just rescued the spoiled daughter of a politician who had no concept of the danger of these mountains. She didn't understand how someone brought up in this country could be so ignorant of the danger. "Let's get moving. The sooner we set off the sooner we'll get to that high valley," she said, more to put a stop to unnecessary thinking than anything else.

They gathered their belongings before setting off without another word between them. Flick was good with that. Maybe it would make the trip more peaceful.

CHAPTER SEVEN

ZAMIRA SAT ON YET another rock and massaged her feet, trying to forget the pain by concentrating on the view. They were high in the mountains, and she was sitting on the top of the world. They were well below the snow line, but there were no trees and the only breaks in the golden yellow of the grass were the rocks standing proud like sentries on the sides of the mountains. She'd taken her boots and socks off, which she'd laid out in the late afternoon sun to dry out. This was the second time today she'd done it, so she could maybe prevent blisters.

Her legs were leaden and when she stood to move across their camp to take care of nature, she nearly dragged them. She wouldn't be able to run to save her life. She'd be lost if someone were to come after them now. She made her way forward with a stiff-legged gait, looking like a TV robot.

Flick emptied one of her bags on the ground. "I'm working out our rations. We have enough pilaw to eat for tonight and some bread for breakfast, but we're almost out of food. I'll catch us a rabbit or goat later."

Zamira stood motionless, unsure she'd heard her correctly. "Did you say catch us a rabbit or goat? Are you going to shoot one? You can't. We already discussed this. You can't shoot something that is a living thing and doing us no damage." Zamira grew more confident. "You can't shoot anything, because the gunshots will mean that anyone up here will know someone else is here. Actually, now I've said that, how can I practice if I can't shoot? It'll draw attention to us—attention we don't want." She looked at Flick smugly. She could win this battle.

Flick stared up at her, and her eyes bored into Zamira. Her face started turning pink, rising from her neck, and then she turned red. Flick stood. "Firstly, we won't use any ammunition when we get you used to a gun, although we'll do drills to practice loading and reloading it." She emphasized every word, speaking as if they were sticking in her throat. "And I'm not going to shoot a rabbit. I'm going to put out some snares and if we're lucky, we may get a rabbit for breakfast. If not, we're going to be hungry on our long and tiring walk tomorrow." She turned back to what she was doing, the conversation clearly over.

Zamira continued walking through the maze of rocks and out of sight of Flick. Flick always had to have the last word, and she had to be right. It was infuriating. First, she was incompetent and now she was being difficult. Zamira had to admit that perhaps she was being a little ungrateful, and she suspected that Flick was an army professional because she'd discussed weapons and survival with ease. She'd put herself at risk to rescue her as well.

She'd vowed after her mumma died that she'd take control of her life, but she'd been out of control since she left the plane. Zamira had to calm down, otherwise she'd be in trouble again. She still hadn't told Flick she didn't eat meat, but she'd cross that bridge later. She took in several gulps of fresh air and concentrated on the view across the valley. It was beautiful, and the kind of place she'd like to walk if she ever made it out of here in one piece. The sun going down created golden shadows across the distant horizon and in another hour, it would be dark. She'd survived another day. She *was* going to make it out of this.

Once she was calm, she returned to their campsite.

"Oh, good, you're here," Flick said. "Shooting practice is next. Come look at my handgun."

Zamira went over and Flick handed it to her, holding the muzzle to the ground and the grip toward her. She took hold of it. Even if it had no ammo in it, she was holding an instrument of death, and she shivered at the thought. How might the world change if there were no guns in it? The power and the ability to launch destruction that came with arms was something that governments always treasured, and it was something she considered studying.

Flick's voice brought her back to the moment. "If you're handed any weapon, there are three things to know. One, always keep the muzzle facing the ground and never toward a person. So, you're doing that. Second, check that the safety is on. Here, it's by the trigger and is on. It means that the weapon cannot fire until the safety is released. Thirdly, open the weapon and check that there isn't a bullet in the chamber. Look inside and ensure there's nothing here, or here. Once you've done that *every* time, you can assume the weapon is safe."

Zamira followed the instructions, hating it but understanding Flick's desire for her to learn. She looked at Flick without saying anything, waiting for more.

"It's a Glock 19, which is common in the Special Operations teams in both the UK and the US. This is the fifth generation, so they've been around a while, and they're considered solid options. It shoots 9mm ammunition and holds fifteen bullets in the magazine plus one in the chamber. I've taken the ammunition out, so don't worry," Flick said. "Now hand it back to me, the way I just showed you."

Zamira sighed and handed it back to Flick. Flick took it and completed the safety checks in seconds. She handed it back to Zamira and ensured she understood what she was doing.

"Now we shoot. I want you to hold the weapon as if you...STOP. DO NOT MOVE A MUSCLE!" Flick said, and Zamira froze. "What were your safety instructions? Never point a weapon at anyone!" Flick said. "Why are you pointing that at me?"

"Well, obviously I wasn't intending to. I was going to shoot over there. But you were in the way as I moved around," Zamira said. She hadn't meant to do anything wrong, but she had to remember a lot, and she hated the weight of it in her hand.

"Oui, madame, I'm sorry I didn't mean to kill your bebe. I was turning around to shoot that bird in the tree." Flick's voice was a high, silly falsetto. "What you did is how mistakes happen. Rarely do people *intend* for accidents to happen."

"Okay, I get it. Don't rub it in. I won't do it again." *Insufferable woman.* Once again, she was on Zamira's case. Although Zamira had to admit, she did seem to know some things.

Flick stood behind her. "We need to get you used to holding the gun in your hand and pulling the trigger. There's no ammo, so it'll only click. You won't get the feel of the kick of a bullet, so we'll compensate. Let's try shooting first. You'll need two hands. Hold the gun in both hands like this."

Flick stood close to her, and Zamira could feel her hips as she leaned around her to put Zamira's hands on the gun. It was warm and somehow, Zamira knew she was safe in those arms. She shook the odd feeling away.

"Make sure you don't put fingers here because the heat in the barrel and the firing pin retracting are dangerous. Squeeze the trigger. Okay, let go. Now have another go. I'll help if you get stuck. If you can do this, then we'll be halfway there. Yes, those fingers there. Perfect."

Flick moved to her side, and it grew cooler behind her. The sense of security that she hadn't felt since she was surrounded by her parents' love was gone. They continued the lesson and ended with Zamira dry-firing at a rock target.

"If you need to fire at a person, you'll just get the gun out, make it ready, and fire. You won't have much time to think about it, so we'll have a little practice each evening," Flick said. "Once you get a magazine loaded in the weapon, the feeling of firing is a lot different. Now when you press the trigger, it just clicks. But when you fire a round, the recoil of the gun will surprise you, and it will knock the weapon upwards. So, what we'll do is get you to aim a bit low. See the rock over there? Aim for about three feet off the ground. Whenever you look at a target aim for that height, don't look at anything else. Think one, two, three feet, and fire."

Zamira's arms ached, and her hands were shaking. Her body hadn't felt great before, but it began to complain loudly. Her legs ached, her stomach grumbled with hunger, and her head hurt from concentrating so hard. She slumped onto the small boulder she'd been standing against. "No more."

Flick took the gun back and stowed it away. "We need to get you fed and then to sleep."

Zamira was unable to do any more than wave a hand at Flick. Once more, even speech wouldn't come. Exhaustion and fear were a potent deterrent to movement of any kind. Flick bent over and picked her up as if she weighed nothing and carried her over to the area they had made to camp for the night. She carefully put Zamira down and wrapped her blanket around her.

"Don't move. I'll make us dinner," Flick said.

Zamira watched her moving around the campsite with her long legs seeming to make the movements effortless. Flick put water in the pan, and Zamira sighed. There was something comforting about a hot drink when you were tired. Green tea was perfect, and she'd been brought up with it. It wasn't the usual fare for Parisians, and she was grateful that Flick had brought it. She couldn't quite bring herself to say thanks out loud though.

Flick brought the pan of tea over to her wrapped in its usual blanket. "I'll be back in a moment. I'm just going to see if I can get us lunch for tomorrow. We'll have our last supplies for supper when I get back." Flick turned around and came back to Zamira. She knelt down and laid a gun on the ground between them. "This weapon has a magazine in it. Now that you can use it, it's there if you need it. Tomorrow, we'll look at how you might carry it, but for now, it's where you can grab it if someone happens to find you while I'm gone. Just don't shoot me," Flick said and laughed. "It would be tough to be friends after that."

Zamira noticed how Flick's face completely changed. Her eyes lit up, and the deep green became like emeralds. There were laughter lines on her face too, which she'd failed to notice. But it was her mouth that had Zamira transfixed. Her serious, thin-lipped mouth turned upwards at the ends, and laughter almost sprang out. It was a heady, instant transformation from severe sergeant major to lighthearted comedian willing to make fun of herself and Zamira.

Within moments, she was serious again and strode off to sort out their food supply. Silence settled around Zamira like a blanket, and she was left alone with the thoughts in her head. She was unravelling inside but wanted to keep a cool appearance so that Flick didn't notice. She'd been terrified ever since she'd been taken, and the continual anxiety was wearing. The thought that maybe even one person may have lost their life made her choke. She cried a few tears feeling sorry for herself. She wasn't important enough for people to die trying to save her. Maybe she should try being more pleasant with Flick because, despite everything, she was the person rescuing her. By the time Flick returned, Zamira had gained control of herself again.

As they settled down for the night, Zamira wondered at how familiar it seemed, yet it was only their second night together. She lay on her side and curled up, and a moment later felt Flick tucking in her blanket around her, followed by Flick's blanket on top. Then Flick's long body curled around hers, giving her warmth and safety. The thought made her breath catch. It had been so long since she'd felt truly safe, and out here, on a mountaintop as they ran for their lives, wasn't exactly a haven. So why did she feel so secure?

***

Zamira became aware that she was cold and that the blackness of the night had changed into gray daylight. She lay on her back watching a cloud passing slowly looking so close, she wanted to touch it. There was no sign of Flick. She was about to see if she could start the tea when Flick reappeared around a rock, making Zamira jump.

"It's me. I was trying not to startle you. I have food."

Zamira swallowed a few times to stop the nausea. Flick had a rabbit in her hand, but she had already skinned it, obviously leaving the mess elsewhere. She held it up for Zamira to see.

"It will take me an hour or so to chop this up and cook it. We'll be able to have a hot meal, and I'll have enough food for us to have lunch and supper today, and maybe breakfast tomorrow." She sighed loudly. "We were lucky. We walked past those rabbits late yesterday, and I guessed their burrow was close. I managed to catch one overnight in a snare, but the chances of it happening as conveniently again are slim. We should enjoy this while we can."

Sweat formed on Zamira's forehead and top lip. "I won't be able to eat it. Just looking at it now is making me feel sick. Even the thought of it turns my stomach," Zamira said. "I'm a vegetarian."

"I'll make us a cup of tea and while the water is heating up, I'll butcher the rabbit," Flick said, already busy with her culinary tasks and seeming to ignore Zamira's comments.

Zamira couldn't watch as Flick took her knife to the rabbit. She wrapped her blanket around her and moved to her rock perch from the night before. Still musing about life and the view in the early dawn, Zamira became aware of Flick standing off to one side with the tea pan.

"When we've finished our tea, I'll start cooking. There's very little out here that you can eat, and you'll need to eat to have energy. You can have my bread and perhaps drink the broth," Flick said and sat down next to Zamira in companionable silence.

Zamira handed her the tea pan when she'd finished her half and Flick started to drink.

"Today and tomorrow, we have some hard walking to do. We're well above the tree line, so the winds here can chill you to the bone. There are few places to shelter, and we don't want to spend a night out on the plains. Once we get to late afternoon, I'll be searching for a gully or some rocks to shelter us for the night. We're going to need every piece of clothing we have, day and night."

Flick didn't seem to need any comment from Zamira as she rose and left.

Cold. Zamira had been brought up in Tarinor but despite living in Denebe and Sayeb, she'd never had much experience of anything more than a walk to school or for shopping in the cold. She was already wearing all her clothing and had a blanket wrapped around her. How would she cope? Would she die up here, making the whole escape worthless?

Flick, meanwhile, seemed to have this survival type of life down fine. Knowing how to survive, getting water, and finding food where there was none. She wasn't inept, not at all, despite Zamira's assertion that she didn't know what she was doing. How did someone get into this kind of life and live it day to day? It wasn't something that you could advertise as a career move. Come and wear yourself out physically, starve unless you can catch something, and deal with whatever the elements have to throw at you. On top of all that, get shot at by random residents of the country you're in. Oh, by the way, did we mention you need to speak the language? She thought back to when she'd first seen Flick outside the prison. She'd spoken to her in three different languages. That had been impressive.

The smell of cooking meat permeated the air. Her stomach betrayed her and rumbled. She was uncertain how she would react if she had to eat it. She was still in denial about her hunger and wanted to eat anything other than something Flick had caught in a snare. But it did smell good.

Zamira walked around the rocks to where Flick had set up the stove in their encampment. The contents of the pan were bubbling away, and Zamira didn't want to look too closely.

Flick beckoned her over. "I've taken the best bits of the rabbit meat and buried the rest, so you won't see anything. I've made rabbit stew with water and some of the herbs that I picked on our travels yesterday. It's not going to be as good as you'd eat at home, but I have figs, rosemary, and wild mint in the water. It should be good enough." Flick stirred the pan with a piece of stick. "I still have a few pieces of stale bread I can soak in water for you, and a couple extra figs, but I'd rather you try to eat some of this. It will help fight the cold and give you enough protein to keep you going."

"I keep retching at the thought. I'll eat the bread," Zamira said, thankful for the last-minute reprieve. She wasn't hungry enough yet to overcome her memory of the skinned rabbit. She knew it was survival of the fittest, and she needed food to be fit. Until the day came when she genuinely had no choice, she'd take the cruelty-free option.

Flick shrugged. "Up to you. I'll take the rest of the stew with us and heat up any leftovers for supper tonight. You'll be hungry by the time we stop again."

Zamira wasn't sure that the effort of carrying leftovers across the high plain in an icy wind would be worth the effort. But it was kind of Flick to offer. Once again, Flick showed her kindness she hadn't earned. Tears filled her eyes, and she turned away. She just wanted her life back.

CHAPTER EIGHT

THEY WERE STILL ALIVE. Not that Flick ever had any doubts about her own survival once they'd made their way into the mountains, but the added complication of someone unused to this sort of environment gave her a good deal of worry. The last thing she wanted to do was lose her target to dehydration, starvation, or because she twisted her ankle and fell over a cliff. It was uneven ground, covered with either sand and small rocks or short grass and clumps of tall grasses. The small boulders everywhere looked like herds of goats in the distance. It was a bizarre, surreal landscape.

The worst thing to cope with was the weather. It was mostly dry and sunny, but the temperature could shift from icy cold to boiling hot in a day. This time of year, it tended to be dry and cold. A constant wind brought the temperature down by several degrees and made walking against it difficult.

They had walked a fair distance, and Flick shivered as they neared a gully with a stream along it. Undoubtedly Zamira would be cold, and they could both do with a hot drink. This would be ideal to refill water containers and have a rest, so she suggested they stop. She washed out their pan in the stream, having transferred the leftover stew into the container Grandmother had given them for mutton stew and set the pan on the stove.

"This may taste a little of stew, but I've cleaned it the best I can using sand from the stream bottom," Flick said. "While it's heating up, let's look at our feet."

"Do we still need to?" Zamira asked.

Flick wondered when Zamira would stop questioning everything she said. "Yes, we do. The cold can make our feet harder to care for, and unless you want to crawl the rest of the way, I suggest you get your boots off."

Once Zamira had her boots and socks off, Flick checked both feet.

The heel on her right foot looked as if it was starting to blister. She'd been keeping an eye on it, but it was getting red. She still had some wild mint in her bag and wondered if it might help if she put a few leaves on it, between Zamira's foot and sock. It might be an old wives' tale in Tarinor that it could help skin infections, but if it worked, it might sort out Zamira's blister.

"Your heel is getting quite red, and I don't want you to suffer in the next couple of days." Flick explained the mint treatment. "Can you watch the tea while I sort out our water bottles?"

Moments later they were sitting barefoot, drinking green tea in the relative shelter of the gully.

"How are you finding the walk today?" Flick said.

"It's really, really hard. I know I'm keeping up with you so far, but I'm not sure I'll last all day. The cold wind is making it difficult," Zamira said.

Flick noted the honesty and lack of attitude and gave silent thanks. "Why don't we make you an extra coat out of your blanket? We can wrap it over your head and shoulders and pull it down to cover your body. If we keep it in place with your belt, it should work. I'll do the same with mine and see if it keeps us warmer," Flick said.

"That's a good idea," Zamira said.

She took her blanket and put it over her head and shoulders. Flick was surprised. For probably the first time since they started out on this journey, Zamira hadn't questioned her at all. Maybe they were reaching an equilibrium. Or maybe Zamira was just too tired to argue.

When they set off, Zamira was protected by her blanket, but the way forward was difficult, and they were moving slow. Flick hadn't bothered to use her blanket yet, but she was suffering from cold hands and wherever she put them, they didn't seem to get warmer. She wore a traditional toki which was a skull cap with a chalma wound around it so that it looked like a turban, and it was keeping her warm for the most part. They walked in silence as usual. If Chalky or Slim had been there, they would have been talking about TV, books, films, and food, specifically chocolate.

She'd lost them both. They'd never be there with her making insane suggestions or making her laugh at herself. She shook her head, trying to clear the thoughts. It didn't work. What they did was always risky, but that was the nature of their work. They trained and trained, improved on their fitness and knowledge so that they could save women like Zamira.

They'd rescued so many over the years, but the cost was high when she kept losing people she cared about. Before the memories swamped her, she started talking.

"Time passes slowly when walking long distances. Makes it hard not to think about how you feel physically. It's good to chat and take your mind off things. My buddies and I used to have long discussions about which was the best beer or chocolate and why. We all loved books too, so we'd swap titles, loves, and likes. Shall we try it?" She almost held her breath waiting for a reply from Zamira. Maybe she found being constantly irritated with Flick preferable.

"Okay, I'll go with that," Zamira said.

Flick pulled her blanket around herself and tightened her belt around it. She put her hands inside for warmth. "Are your hands cold?"

"Yes, they've been getting colder as the day has gone on," Zamira said.

"Put them inside your blanket. It can make you feel a little unbalanced, but it's worth it. Just take it easy when you walk."

Zamira did as Flick suggested and smiled slightly. "That should work, thank you." She moved to Flick's side. "I'll start by asking a question. Who do you work for? Who sent you for me?"

It was a logical place to start, but Flick wasn't at liberty to share that information. The conversation was going to come unstuck very quickly. "I work for a little-known department in the UK."

"It sounds like something out of one of those books you love to read," Zamira said.

Flick laughed more out of nervousness than anything else. How to tell a story while saying nothing? "We're a small team, mostly women, who can speak several languages and easily fit in many countries without standing out. We rescue women in trouble like you from all over the world."

"How do you find them?"

"Through contacts, government, the media. Wherever there's a need."

"And you enjoy what you do?"

There seemed to be no judgment in Zamira's tone, just real curiosity. Flick hesitated. "I did—I do. I don't know right now. This job changes you."

"I can understand that it would, having been here with you." Zamira looked up at her. "Until two years ago, I was just an ordinary Tarin girl studying at university. Then my world changed, and I find it hard to relate to the girl I used to be."

"How are you different?"

"I had to become more independent and survive in a different country. Until then, telling anyone about myself had always been easy. I had a happy family life. Since then, it's been hard and will be even harder after this." She kicked at a rock and stumbled, and Flick stepped in front of her to steady her. Zamira nodded her thanks. "Why did you come on this mission? To get me?"

Again, it wasn't a simple question, but Flick wanted to be part of a more involved discussion and one-word answers wouldn't work for that. "I lost someone dear to me, and I was promoted out of the field. I've spent the last year or so sitting at a desk watching the clock. I've struggled to deal with the day to day of an office. When the chance came up to get back in the field, I took it. But..." Flick closed her eyes against the wave of pain. "I'll get to the difficult bit later. I'll work up to it," she said.

Zamira shot her a look of sympathy, and Flick turned away, quickening her step slightly to put Zamira behind her. She looked around at the grass, rocks, and the high mountain peaks and recognized how divorced this world was from the one she lived in. The freshness on that icy wind, with overtones of soil, and rock, and goat was a world away from city traffic. And the noise of the wind racing across the plain was nothing compared to sirens, traffic, and pedestrian shouts and whistles. Yet it some ways, the desolation mirrored the emptiness of her world and in contrast, the traffic signaled how much the world moved on without her.

"What about your family?" Zamira asked. "You know about mine."

Yet another sore spot. Maybe talking hadn't been a good idea after all. "I was brought up in the UK. My family are farmers, and we have a lot of land, so I'll never be penniless," Flick said. "Neither will my three older brothers."

"Does your father run the farm on his own, or do your brothers help?"

Flick looked across at her. She seemed to be engaging with the conversation and looked interested. At this rate the journey would pass quickly. "The farm has been in my family for generations. My father takes a bit more of a back seat these days and tends to deal with horses. My two oldest brothers run the farm. It's a long story how I ended up here."

"I'm curious now. How do you get to be a rescuer and survival expert when your father is a farmer?"

Her recruitment was another thing she couldn't talk about. "My three brothers are the best thing about my life. I'd do everything they did. I climbed, fished, and created mayhem on the family farm alongside them. Those were happy days." She continued looking around her. "I think we should stop for a rest in the next hour. What do you think? How cold are you?"

"You're right. Chatting does take your mind off the cold and the walking. I'm doing okay. There are some goats up ahead that look like a herd. Will they have a goat herder, do you think?" Zamira asked.

Flick looked to where Zamira pointed. Flick hoped not. She didn't want more complications. She could see the herd, but they looked unattended. "Let me know if you see anyone. We don't want to advertise that we're walking across here," Flick said.

"Tell me about a good memory you have from those days," Zamira said.

"Like I said, I did everything with my brothers. Mama gently suggested that I should wear a dress to go to church on Sunday. I was nine and ran away. I could have disagreed or argued with her, but I wasn't going to do it and used my legs to make the point instead. Mama eventually found me at the back of a disused stable on the farm, sound asleep with a stray dog in my arms." Flick smiled at the memory, and warmth spread through her body. She could still feel the wiry hair of Jack, that old stray, and the smell of dog as she laid her head on his body. "I like being a woman, but I don't have to wear a dress to be one as is expected by society. And I like women too." She laughed. She *loved* women, and she'd had some wonderful times with them. They were a part of her essence. She knew how to look after a woman and give her the world. Just like she had Leah. *No. No. No. We're not traveling this road again.*

"So, anyway, Papa spent time in the military. He's loving but distant. He treats me like one of his boys, and we get along just fine. Papa's considered by outsiders as taciturn and only speaks when necessary or when situations expect it of him." Flick paused as she tried to gather her thoughts. She hadn't talked this much about her family in a long time. A visit was overdue. "He met my mama in the Army. She's the complete opposite. She's Italian and fiery, with flashing eyes and lots of smiles."

"Is that where you get yours from?"

Flick's eyebrow quirked, and she grinned. "I suppose, although I think I've been incredibly calm with you. My brothers mostly take after my father, and I have his height. But for the rest, I'm all my mother." Flick was proud of her Italian heritage.

"So is your name really Flick?"

"Why? Do I look like a Felicity to you?" Flick asked as she twirled on the path.

"Um, no, you don't." Zamira said.

Flick walked ahead a little and then slowed down, lost in thought.

"If your mother is Italian and your father is in the British Army, how did they meet?"

"She met Papa at a diplomatic dinner in London when she was working at the Italian embassy for their chief military attaché. Papa was a colonel in the Royal Engineers. Mama tells the story of arriving at the Painted Hall in Greenwich and being astounded at the way it was lit by candlelight and spotlight, showing off the wonderful ceiling. It had always been thought of as the English version of the Sistine Chapel. Some two hundred people sat down to dinner, and she found herself next to a handsome but quiet officer in a bright red jacket. She managed to get him chatting, and they discussed horses and dogs that they owned. By the time the after-dinner entertainment was on, they were like old friends. Papa asked for her phone number, and so began their relationship. They fell deeply in love." She loved her parents, but she was their youngest, and the only girl, and had found their expectations difficult. Not only did she fight against wearing a dress when she was a child, but once she grew up, she didn't want to marry a man. Although they all knew she was gay and had met Leah when they were together, she worried that she hadn't met the expectations of her very traditional family and because of that, she had rarely visited home with her. She understood family responsibility, but she needed her independence.

"How did your papa end up as a farmer?" Zamira asked.

"When he was in the army, he and Mama moved to his postings with us. But Grandpop died, and Papa had to take over the farm. We moved to Norfolk and then had lots of room to run free."

"And that worked for you?"

"Oh, yeah. My parents were busy running things so as I grew up, I managed to stay outside a lot and well, as they said at the time, I was a little wild." Flick took her hands out of her blanket and gestured around them. "I got worse as I got older, staying outdoors so I didn't have to learn to do cooking, and sewing, and whatever it is young teenage girls were supposed to learn."

"I was wondering how you ended up living a life where you're free in the outdoors, and you have just explained it to me. Wild and away from the house," Zamira said.

"Sadly, it ended when I was sent to school in Switzerland. I didn't want to go, but they convinced me I could go canoeing, mountain climbing, and skiing, and also have the chance to do one of the few things I'm good at, learning languages." Flick bundled herself up again.

"Yes, I noticed. When we first met, you tried three different ones, and you've been speaking excellent French since we met. How many languages can you speak?"

"Nine or ten, but one or two, like Tarin, aren't quite perfect. The army taught me a couple they wanted me to use. Then I ended up using them doing what I do best, helping to rescue damsels in distress." Flick laughed again, and her heart filled with joy. Talking to Zamira must have been good for her. They'd been walking for a while, and the time had passed much more quickly than their earlier silent walk. "I think I've talked through lunch, but we should have a rest and a hot drink before going on to dusk. What do you think?"

Zamira looked at her. "What do I think? I think that's a good idea, and thank you for asking."

Flick wondered if she'd been barking instructions and not asking Zamira's opinion. But in her defense, they hadn't had an easy start to their relationship. They continued walking after a brief stop to eat, and there was no sign of any tribesmen or goatherders. Flick was relieved. More complications weren't necessary. Just as she was celebrating the fact, she heard the familiar beating blades of a low-flying helicopter.

"Get down in the rocks and don't look up," she shouted to Zamira. She shoved her into a gap and lay face down. Being chased across the mountains by the president's men in a helicopter was the worst-case scenario. Not for the first time in her life, she prayed. She wasn't religious as such but accepted that there was a higher being who may or may not help in times of severe stress. Since Leah's death, she wasn't certain there was anyone who might help, but they were in a perilous position and any assistance would be welcome.

The helicopter came closer, the heavy bass beat of the rotors moving through the air and getting louder. Sand and pebbles flew around them like small missiles, crashing against the boulders. Flick heard the much higher whine of the engine as the chopper came closer. Her heart was beating almost in time with the rotor, getting faster and louder as the chopper moved toward them. After far too long, the sound lessened and moved away.

She let out the breath she'd been holding. Just as Flick raised her head, the noise grew louder again, and the chopper returned. She ducked down again, hoping that Zamira had done likewise. The chopper crew were obviously looking closely at the herd of goats to see if there were any humans amongst it. The herd, spooked by the noise, ran and revealed there was no one on two legs in their midst. The chopper flew off, its sound echoing off the mountains for a long time.

"Don't move for a while," Flick said, lying motionless. "They may come back. It's a race for them to find us before we get out of the country. I'm hoping they think we followed the road out of Sayeb, the one we crossed yesterday, and are concentrating their main forces on that. The media will soon realize that there hasn't been a third press briefing, so the president will be frantic. All hell is probably breaking loose out there." Flick didn't mention that her own organization may think that she was dead too. No doubt word had gotten back about the downed helo and English operatives on board.

They crawled out of the rocks after another half hour. Zamira hadn't said a word the whole time. "You okay?" Flick asked, dusting herself off.

"No." Zamira's voice was soft. "I told myself we were. That we just had to take a long walk and then we'd be safe." She brushed tears away from her eyes. "But they could still catch me. They could still send me back to prison or kill me on camera to break my father's will."

Flick studied the ground, uncertain what to say. Zamira was only speaking truth. "Let's get going."

As dusk turned the sky a pale, dusty orange, they moved toward the edge of the plain. There were numerous rocky outcrops, and Flick hoped for a good selection of shelter for the night. They found a good spot out of the worst of the wind. Flick heated up their fig and rabbit stew and understood how hungry Zamira must be when she agreed to eat her portion. The cold and hard exercise would have exhausted her, and Flick needed to ensure that Zamira ate. She wiped out the pan with some grass and started to heat some water for some tea. Hot food and tea would help them stay warm for some of the night.

Once she'd made tea, Flick sat down next to Zamira and wrapped her blanket around them both. The warmth of their mugs and their closeness under the blanket would help to keep the cold at bay.

"When you told me your story, you said you'd lost someone. Will you tell me about them?" Zamira asked.

Flick stiffened. She wasn't sure she could do this. She hadn't talked to anyone about it. Zamira didn't look at her and continued staring into the gathering darkness. Somehow it helped. There was something impersonal about talking in the dark to a stranger and knowing that no one could see the tears.

"It was my wife. It still hurts. It happened over two years ago, but sometimes it seems like only yesterday. We had a whirlwind life together. I'd just left the Army when we met in Afghanistan and was doing some undercover work and training before joining my new department. Leah was doing intelligence work in the main control center for military operations in Afghanistan. We hit it off, and we had something special. I did three more ops in Afghanistan before she came home to the UK. We were married within months, although we were both working and traveling here and there. We spent every free moment we could steal together. I spent a lot of nights driving home from somewhere to spend a few hours with her before she had to get up early to go to a briefing or whatever."

Her stomach twisted, as did the knife in her heart. "Leah received a second posting to Afghanistan, back to central operations to continue her intelligence role. She cried when she told me. She loved her work but was all set to give it up so that we could stay together in the UK. But I was starting to get involved in the department, and I was traveling to complete operations all over the world. If she stayed in the UK, I was likely to be away a lot. I convinced her to go. We had a few days together and then she was gone. I never saw her again. She was killed by a mine while on a humanitarian mission. She was helping a village, for God's sake. She didn't have a violent bone in her body. She wasn't at all combative. Why did she have to die? Why did I convince her to go? I thought she'd be safe." She would never lose the guilt. She'd told Leah to go. It was her fault. Flick turned away from Zamira and curled up in the smallest ball that she could, like a stone in the middle of a peach, hard and protected from the outside world.

Flick was empty. She had no one to blame but herself for convincing Leah to go. She could rage against the Taliban, God, the government, and anyone else she could think of, but it was her. She had convinced Leah to go and not to stay at home waiting for her return from operations across the world.

Zamira curled behind Flick and held her tight. Flick became aware of her whispering to her in Tarin. "Hush, my baby. It will be all right. Life will be good again soon. Remember those happy times. It's not your fault. She loved her job and would have been unfulfilled without it."

Flick closed her eyes and, feeling strangely comforted, she fell asleep in Zamira's embrace.

CHAPTER NINE

WHEN ZAMIRA AWOKE, HER back was chilled, and Flick was curled up in her arms. It was light, so she must have slept through the night. She hadn't fully awoken, but she was conscious that she'd been cold. She now understood how Flick had been caring for her. Last night, she hadn't been tucked in to keep her warm, and nor did she have her own and Flick's blankets. She'd also had strange dreams about monsters with guns and men hiding in gullies.

Flick turned over so they were lying face to face. Zamira felt the heat rising to her cheeks and watched as Flick seemed to be having a similar reaction.

"Good morning," Flick said.

"Good morning," Zamira said. She didn't know if she should address Flick's confession and outpouring last night or not.

"I'm sorry to have given you a torrent of all my worries. That's not happened to me before. I'm obviously tired and losing my friends has brought it all back to me. I'm sorry," Flick said. "It was incredibly unprofessional." She looked up to the sky as she spoke.

"Please don't be embarrassed. I'm honored that you trusted me enough to speak to me about Leah. I would have loved to have known her. You were obviously a happy couple," Zamira said. "And you can look at me again. I'll think I've grown another head if you can't look at me," Zamira said.

Flick turned and looked at her with a half-smile. "Thank you," she said and stood. "I'll go and check our snares, although I'm not hopeful."

Zamira lay with the extra blanket and thought about Flick and her hurt and guilt. She'd been carrying a heavy weight. Had no one told her that her guilt was part of her slanted view? That she was actually feeling guilty because she was still alive and Leah had gone. Flick was left with their plans and dreams, their hopes for the future, and they'd all been shattered. Zamira understood some of this. When her mother had gone,

Zamira's thoughts of the future changed, and she'd had her own hopes and dreams shattered. She was still entrenched in those thoughts and feelings, and she still held her father responsible. She had to release the tension that invaded her body the moment she thought of him.

"Are you okay?"

Her thoughts were broken by Flick as she returned with wire in her hands.

"Yes, fine." She unclenched her fists and stood, her body stiff and sore.

"Sorry, no breakfast this morning. We still have some green tea, or we can have mint tea if you like. I have a few leaves in my bag, although they aren't too fresh."

"Green tea is fine. I must admit I'm quite hungry this morning," Zamira said.

"Me too. We've done quite well so far. I was considering killing a goat, but to be honest, we're not that desperate yet. It wouldn't be easy. To build a trap would take time that we don't have," Flick said as she poured water into their pan. "We'll make our way to the edge of the plain today. Later this afternoon, we'll start our descent, so it'll get warmer. There'll be more mountain streams, and maybe I can set a snare tonight so we can have a hot breakfast tomorrow before we cross into Pakistan."

Zamira heard what Flick didn't say: that it would also become more dangerous because more people would be around.

They drank their tea before moving out into the biting cold wind once again. Zamira watched the ground ahead. Moss in clumps, small rocks, then a clump of longer grass to walk around and more rocks. It was nothing like walking in a park in Paris. She missed it, and this terrain only brought with it the difficult memories of childhood.

Zamira wanted to share her mother's disappearance with Flick so that the slight awkwardness in the interactions this morning wouldn't be one-sided. She couldn't understand exactly why she wanted to share this with her, but it seemed right. She took a deep breath. "I lost my mumma two years ago, and I don't think I'll ever recover," Zamira said.

Tears formed in Zamira's eyes and ran down her cheeks despite the wind. Flick moved forward and put her arms around her. She drew her close, and Zamira pushed up against her, happy to take the comfort Flick was offering.

"When I suggested we chat, I didn't think we'd end up discussing losing people close to us," Flick said. "Not exactly lighthearted, is it?"

She reluctantly pulled away from Flick and felt a mental as well as physical separation.

"We can carry on chatting, but let's move or we'll get cold," Flick said, almost scooping Zamira up in her left arm and pulling her along with her. "Tell me about your mother. I want to know what makes her so special."

"That's the thing about Mumma. She was special to me, but she was just an ordinary woman. She was brought up in Denebe, and her father was an administrator. She did things any girl would do, went to school, liked fashion, and things like that. She met and fell in love with my father when she was eighteen. And then her life started changing." Her mind was full of rage, and she seethed with the loss and waste. "I hate him, it's his fault. This is all his fault," she said. She'd freed her hands from her blanket and waved her arms around, needing some way to let these feelings out. "My father had all these ideals when he was younger, and they haven't changed. The big difference is that his younger ideas were just that—ideals. But as he got older, he realized that he had the ability to put them into practice, that the corruption in the institutions of Tarinor could be cleaned up, could be stopped, and he had the power to do that. He did good work in getting the education system to work more on merit and less on money. I went to schools based on my ability, although my father was wealthy enough to pay and powerful enough to use his influence. He wanted all children to have the same choices that I had."

"There are private schools in the UK, but it's possible to get an excellent education in the state system, and that's based on merit. It sounds like your father's heart is in the right place. What happened for him to meet the Lyulli?" Flick asked.

"He tried to put a stop to the network created by money-grabbing politicians. Drug money was a serious problem. Politicians decided to blame the Lyulli for the drugs that were spreading all over the country, and they were getting international pressure to clamp down on them. What I didn't understand at the time was that the government was accepting money from drug contacts abroad to turn a blind eye to the whole disgusting system. When the international pressure became difficult to counteract, the president publicly blamed the Lyulli."

"Ah, it's starting to make sense now," Flick said. "Your father went against the president and then his trouble really started."

"Yes. As you know, they're nomads. My father stood up for the Lyulli and pointed out to the world that they've never dealt in drugs and that drugs don't form a part of their culture. My father pointed out loudly and publicly that people who are outside the mainstream of Tarin culture make good scapegoats."

"Not just in Tarinor," Flick said.

"Yes, so I'm learning. He then investigated the finances of several politicians, including the president, and found they had new houses and cars, had been on expensive holidays overseas, and were spending money on lavish entertaining. It was at this time my mother disappeared."

Zamira walked in a dreamlike state. Her memories were raw. She'd never spoken to anyone about the events surrounding her mumma's death. She drew in a breath, then another. She could do this. It would be good to let it all out and talk about it.

"Damn," Flick said.

"I'd gone to school and my father to work. On Tuesdays, Mumma visited her parents to help them out, cleaning, cooking, and things. But she never arrived. When I came home from school, she wasn't there, so I went to my grandparents' house. They told me they thought she was ill as she hadn't come to see them. I went home and waited for my father. He came home and didn't know where she was. I went to all her friends, and my father talked to all the neighbors around us." She took a deep, shuddering breath. "One of the neighbors had seen her getting into a black government car. We never saw her again."

Zamira was reminded of that day and the hope that she had that her mother had just gone somewhere to help the government and would be back in a few hours. Despite her own logic and knowledge that her mother didn't care about politics, she'd still hoped that she'd return.

Her father had been frantic. She'd never seen him like that. He was rushing here and there, all the while sweating and panicking. He came and went from their home. He went to his office and came home again. Zamira was there, but he didn't seem to see her. Mumma's parents came round and sat with her as they waited.

"Eventually, after two days my father stood before us. By then, he was gray-faced. He'd had no sleep, and tears ran down his face. 'The president was involved, but I can't prove it. She's not coming back. She's dead. My beautiful and darling wife, your daughter, and your mumma, has been stolen from us,' he said to us all. There was no proof. No note, no body. But when people disappear in government cars, they don't come back." It hurt to breathe, and Zamira felt the weight of the memory like an anchor in feathers. "He said, 'My work has killed her. I believed that we could change things in Tarinor. She shared my dream that life could be better for ordinary people. She didn't deserve this. You didn't deserve this. It's all my fault.' He cried, and I had trouble understanding him, but his pain was real. 'They're going to come after me now and that means you too, Zamira. We should leave and go somewhere safe.'" Zamira looked at Flick, who was frowning deeply as she listened. "I can still remember the whole conversation, word for word. I replay it in my sleep. I raged at him. I said, 'You killed her. You could've just stuck a knife in her heart. It would have had the same effect. You're a murderer. I'm not going anywhere with you.'" Zamira was spitting as she spoke. "He wanted to go to the US or somewhere in Europe. Anywhere would be safer than Tarinor. But I refused to go with him. I spoke to my professor and found somewhere to continue studying. I refused to have anything else to do with him. As far as I was concerned, he'd murdered Mumma. I went to Paris alone and made my own way. Most people know I'm from Tarinor but nothing else."

Flick held up her hand to stop them. They'd reached the edge of the plain and the stream they'd been following disappeared between some rocks. As they got closer, they could hear the sound of falling water, and despite her inner emptiness, Zamira was at once enchanted by the thought of water leaping over rocks. Perhaps it could wash away some of the pain.

Flick was ahead of her. "Come and sit for a moment out of the wind. This view and the sound of the water are mesmerizing," she called over her shoulder.

Flick was right. Zamira could see for miles across the low hills. In other directions, more mountains continued the range that was behind them. In a way, it had been good to talk about Mumma disappearing and how angry she was with her father. She'd had all those feelings inside but hadn't been close enough to anyone to discuss it. She wasn't close to Flick, though, so why was this different? They'd both been open about their feelings as they'd crossed the plains in that biting wind. Maybe it was all about letting go with a stranger that you'd never see again, like an anonymous outpouring. It wasn't going to catch up with her anytime soon. She and Flick would go their separate ways, and these intimate moments would be forgotten. Zamira doubted she'd ever forget Flick curled in a ball with guilt and loss for Leah and how she'd curled up behind her and comforted her.

Flick pointed to a narrow valley in the distance. "We'll go down there next; it'll take us to the border eventually. That's the only way. If we wanted to avoid the border checkpoint, we'd have to go higher and through snow this time of year," she said. "I'll refill our flasks while we have fresh water. I still have tablets left so even if we're hungry, we'll have plenty of water. Once we're through the border, we have about a day's walk to the shell of a herder's hut. I'll make a call, and we'll be picked up shortly afterward."

Flick was sharing more details about their journey and though she wasn't asking her opinion, Zamira was sure it was part of the way their relationship was changing.

"There may be some fruit bushes when we get lower down the mountains. We need another find like that fig bush," Flick said.

Zamira could still taste that rabbit stew with figs. Though she was hungry, her feelings of nausea around the dead rabbit rose again. "Never mind the figs, do you think there's a pizza shop down there?" she asked, keeping her eyes on Flick. She wanted to see if Flick laughed and how it would transform her face. She wasn't disappointed.

Flick laughed and turned to face her. Her teeth were white and straight, and they highlighted the redness of her lips.

"Come on, let's get going," Flick said. "The sooner we get off this mountain, the sooner you'll get your pizza."

They set off downhill and for the first time in days were out of the cold wind. It was no easier underfoot, and the trek exercised muscles Zamira had forgotten she possessed. It was different but just as challenging. As they neared the pass, Zamira could see the goats perilously close to the edge of almost nonexistent pathways across the wall-like cliffs.

"We need to be careful as we go through the pass. There's a good chance of a random rockfall caused by goats or other animals above," Flick said. Zamira followed Flick's gaze up to the top of the pass hundreds of feet above her. "There's also the chance that the Tarin police or presidential security guessed that we came this way and want to solve their problem with us under a pile of stones. We need to keep our wits about us."

That was more than frightening. Having someone you can see chasing you was one thing. But the rising hair on the back of her neck and a sudden cold flash caused her to shiver. Someone could be up there willing to take their lives. Even if they weren't the people chasing them, they could be random drug smugglers, kidnappers, or goats. Flick had been through these mountains already and been shot out of the sky by someone unknown. She must have deep courage to do it again.

Zamira walked along at the start of the pass, trying not to trip as she stared up. By not looking at her footing, she risked an injury. The floor of the pass was rock and shale, with the ubiquitous clumps of longer grass, browning in the seemingly waterless landscape. She tripped and had to catch herself on the jagged rock beside her.

"You need to watch your footing," Flick said. "We'll slow down a bit so we can keep our eyes open. If you catch a movement and you're not sure, tell me. I don't mind stopping to see what it might be."

A short while later, Flick put her hand out in front of Zamira and stopped her. "I thought I saw something up there. Let's wait a moment," Flick said softly, taking her hand away. She waited a moment but nothing happened. "Okay, false alarm."

They walked for some time when Zamira caught a movement out of the corner of her eye from way above. "Flick, I think there are several goats above us. Lookout!"

There was a loud cracking noise and rumbling. Flick turned toward her. Before Zamira could do anything, Flick ran at her and plucked her up in her arms, propelling her to the side. Flick carried her to an overhang. The sky rained rocks, and Flick pushed her up against the cliff wall on the opposite side of the pass and put her body over Zamira's. She was conscious of Flick's hard breathing, and her chest expanding and contracting against her own. It was hot, suffocatingly so. Flick's body jerked as stones hit her, but she didn't make a sound.

The rocks continued to fall, and they pressed together until the rumbling and banging noise finally stopped, and there was silence. Neither she nor Flick moved. There was a clatter, and a single rock bumped to the ground.

Flick raised her head. "We need to be careful. There'll still be an odd rock or two falling."

Flick rose slowly, and the air around Zamira cooled. Flick pushed through the covering of rocks and stones that covered her as if they were bird feathers. They clattered as they skittered away. Zamira brushed the rock dust off her body. She started to brush Flick's arms but didn't want to brush her back until she'd checked for any injuries. Zamira was once again aware how Flick automatically protected her. She'd never had that happen before.

"Let me look at your back," she said, holding on to Flick's arm.

Flick stared at her. "No, it'll be okay. It's likely to be bruised, but I'll survive," Flick said, looking over her shoulder at Zamira. "It's nothing to worry about."

Zamira wasn't going to be dissuaded. "You may think you're okay, but if one of those rocks broke the skin, then you might be bleeding and won't notice. I'd like to check. Let's get on with it, then we can move on. Please."

Flick stared at her. Zamira wondered if she were deciding whether she could get away with it.

"Fine, but let's go to flat ground over there." Flick indicated an area that was untouched by the rockfall.

Once she'd reached the area, she started taking her upper clothes off. With a jacket, waistcoat, shirt, and vest, there were a lot of layers. She had turned away, but Zamira could see the defined muscles in her upper shoulders and arms. Flick began unwinding the binding wrapped around her.

"It's to keep my breasts hidden," Flick said as she undid it.

Zamira looked at Flick's back. There was a cut on one shoulder which wasn't bad enough to do more than bleed a little, and it would clot quickly. The rest of her back was going to be badly bruised. It had already started to look red and purple in places.

"We're going to need a stream or river. I want to get cold water onto your back to help with the swelling. You only have a slight cut, so that's the good news," Zamira said. She couldn't take her eyes off Flick's back. Despite the redness in places, and the newly formed bruises, it was beautifully toned. Zamira couldn't resist putting her hand on it. Flick turned quickly at Zamira's action and took in a deep breath. She clutched her clothes in her arms, but Zamira could see quite a bit of the front of Flick's naked torso. Even disheveled and dirty, she exuded strength and sensuality. Zamira held Flick's bare arm. Her body made her wonder about curling up with her naked instead of being clothed. She became aware of Flick looking at her strangely. She took her hand away and felt the color rising in her cheeks. She turned away quickly.

"The place I had in mind to camp tonight isn't far from a stream, so we can sort my back out then," Flick said, although her initial couple of words had a strangled kind of sound.

Maybe Flick wasn't unaware of her either. Zamira could hear a strange whimpering sound coming from farther in the rockfall. She hesitated to move toward it, but Flick was by then fully dressed and came alongside her.

"I heard it too," she said. "I think it may be a goat. You saw them before the fall."

They moved toward the sound and sure enough, a young kid was lying with smashed front legs, and it looked as if it was bleeding to death.

"Leave me here with the goat, Zamira. It's not going to recover so I'll put it out of its misery."

Zamira was about to dry heave again. She put her hand toward the goat and wished it a better life in its new world. She climbed back to the flat ground. There was a murmur from Flick and a crack of rock. Then there was silence. Flick came and joined her. She had some blood spattered on her face and jacket.

"I know you don't want to hear this, but we're starving, and that goat has meat we can use. It's not pizza, but I expect you've had goat before in Tarinor, maybe before you became vegetarian?"

"When I was a child, I had goat stew, cooked long and slow over a low heat with lots of flavorings and onions. But a dead baby goat on the mountainside makes me want to cry out in pain for the baby and its mother, who may be up on the top there looking for it," Zamira said.

"I'm afraid we're short on the flavorings, but I think that it was only a few months old, so was still being fed by its mother. It means the meat will be tender and not as stringy as an older animal. If we cook it in water, even without anything else, I think we should get a reasonable stew. We have just about enough petrol left for the rest of the journey. If we're unlucky, we may have to do without tea later on, but I think we should have plenty of water, and I still have tablets left."

There was the military version of Flick she'd seen since the beginning. Logical, planning, non-emotional. It must be nice to detach that way. Zamira had never been so close to decisions that affected her health personally, or life or death for some defenseless animal. For the first time, she could really understand why she was a vegetarian.

"I'll go ahead and cut some pieces of goat for us. I can use the container I used for the rabbit stew. I'll cover up the carcass after. If anyone comes down here and finds the rockfall, they won't know that anyone was here, or if they're looking for us, they may think we didn't survive. We need to get moving down the pass by nightfall."

Flick put her handgun in her trousers and went back to the carcass of the young goat with her knife and the container while Zamira wandered farther down the pass with Flick's bags. She found shelter between two rocks in the sun and closed her eyes for a moment. This was the first time since she'd left the prison that she'd sat in the sun and rested.

A shadow fell across her, and she was aware that the sun was going from this part of the pass.

"Are you ready to move on?" Flick asked.

"Not really, but we need to get home and sitting here in the sun won't help that," Zamira said.

"We can sit in the sun and wait when we get to the RV point while we wait for the helo. We need to keep moving until then. The less time we spend in these mountains, the better." Flick pulled Zamira to her feet. She put the food container in one of the bags, picked both bags up and set off. "I expect from here that we'll find people watching for us."

"Why here?" Zamira asked.

"The president would know it was pointless trying to follow us across the mountains, even if he was close enough to track us. All he has to do is to man the checkpoints at the border on the other side."

"Surely there are quite a few border checkpoints," Zamira said.

"You'd think so. But there are only a dozen checkpoints in the hundreds of miles of border here. Most of the border is in the high mountains and it would be pointless for anyone except hardened explorers and climbers to take that route. Unfortunately, we're neither of those." Flick scanned the pass. "The other thing the president might consider doing is sending police or tribesmen up from the checkpoint and into the mountains. It would take a day or two to get a force from Denebe to the border calling in at Sayeb, but that could be a viable alternative for them."

"It sounds as if we're going to have all sorts of problems and people after us," Zamira said. It wasn't surprising, and really, she didn't need to be told. But filling the silence was better than walking with fear.

"We're going to follow a goat track out of the pass so we don't exit at the far end, right in front of the checkpoint. We need to allow plenty of time because the route is difficult, and we have to get under cover by nightfall. I want us to arrive at the border just before dawn, when the light isn't good and the night lights on the border have just switched off. The guards are tired at that point too. The timing has to be perfect." Flick said.

"We should start climbing soon," Zamira said. The thought made her soul ache. What she wouldn't give for a hot bath and a bed that wasn't made of rocks.

"Yes. There's a sharp bend in the pass and about a mile beyond it is an old rockfall. We'll climb up the large rocks at back of it, and that'll take us onto the goat path. From there, we'll make our way down the pass. We need to keep our eyes open for anything unusual or odd noises. But this is our best way forward." She glanced over her shoulder and gave Zamira a quick smile. "We'll take it steady, and we'll get you home."

Zamira had managed to survive this far, and she hoped that her escort continued to be as resourceful and caring. If only they were spending romantic time in the mountains instead of being hunted. Maybe they could be friends if they made it out of this alive. She thought of Flick's arms and back and shivered. *Just friends.*

CHAPTER TEN

SHE'D HAD LITTLE SLEEP and was starting to feel tired. Rest had to be sacrificed to keep Zamira safe. "I'm going to run ahead for half a mile down the pass and leave some marks at the side of the trail just in case someone follows us down. I want them to think that's the way we've gone. I'll be back soon. I've left you all the gear so perhaps make us a cup of tea and get your boots off," Flick said. She'd already turned to leave. Being followed was unlikely, given that the helicopter search had been fruitless, but Flick liked to have all her bases covered, and to ignore the obvious wasn't in her character. From here on out, things would only get more dangerous, and she needed to be at the top of her game.

"Please be safe. I don't want to get stuck here on my own," Zamira said. "I don't...I don't know what I'd do without you."

Flick turned back to her. "I won't take any risks, and I'll be back before you've finished drinking your tea." She set off, keeping an eye out for any signs of other people while also formulating plan after plan, should things go sideways.

They continued their trek along the goat path once Flick returned. She'd drunk the tea Zamira had made and a lot of water. It was hot in the pass, and she didn't want to get dehydrated. They reached a small mountain stream that crossed their path and disappeared underground through a dry crack, like tears falling into the earth. They filled up their water bottles, and Flick repacked their bags.

"You need to get your clothes off," Zamira said, standing with her hands on her hips.

In any other place on Earth, that statement would have made Flick smile and agree wholeheartedly. But Zamira's tone brooked no argument, and it definitely wasn't flirtatious. Flick rolled her eyes. They didn't have enough time. Didn't Zamira understand that? "We have to keep moving. There's quite a way to go before it gets dark. I don't want us to be on this track when there's not enough light," Flick said.

"Well, you need to strip quickly then. You need to put the whole of the back of your body into the water to get those bruises some relief. I've seen you wincing. Come on, get moving."

The truth was her back hurt her like the devil had taken a paddle to it. Every bit ached. But where the packs pressed, it was far worse. "Fine." With far more petulance than was necessary, she stripped again, and Zamira made no move to turn around. She had spent her life in communal living and the military, and she'd never thought twice about stripping in front of other people, but this was different. There was no way she was embarrassed in front of Zamira. She was someone to be rescued, nothing more. And yet, she turned around to remove her clothes.

Zamira came and stood at her side. "Give me your clothes. I'll hold onto them," she said.

Flick wasn't going to win anything here by being stubborn. She unwound her band and removed it. She removed her trousers and her shorts and stood naked. Before she could think about it, she walked to the stream and lay down with her back in the cold water, letting it flow over her. Zamira was right; she did need this. Her back and legs were badly bruised, and the cold water on them was a relief.

Zamira held her clothing and continued to stare at Flick. Finally, her eyes reached Flick's, and she smiled. Flick's nipples were hard with the cold, but the rest of her body was hot after that examination and smile. She ignored her body. It had no say in this. "Can I come out now? I'm turning to ice in here," Flick said.

"Yes, of course. Has it helped?" Zamira held out Flick's blanket to dry herself with.

Flick shook herself like a puppy, spraying ice-cold water droplets over Zamira.

"Ah! I know I need a shower and I smell, but that won't be enough. I'll need soap and lots of hot water to get anything clean." Zamira brushed at the water.

"I know. At least your dust hasn't solidified into mud." Flick laughed and put on her shorts and trousers. Her unusual embarrassment had gone, and she was quite comfortable. It was a rescue. They often required operatives to leave behind their dignity. Still, she'd need to think through her reactions when she had a moment. She'd never crossed a line with a rescued woman. All professional, all the time. But with Zamira, things were somehow different.

Zamira stood behind her. "It looks like your shoulders and upper back took the brunt of the rockfall. The rest doesn't look as bad. Do you need a hand with your breast band?" Zamira held out the binding.

Flick shook her head, took the breast binding from Zamira and flattened away the evidence of her being a woman. As she did it, she mentally moved back into her Tarin persona and Department Six undercover operative mentality. Put on the disguise, become the person, get the job done. "Let's move out. We need to move quickly and quietly and keep our eyes and ears open."

They didn't speak much as they traveled. Flick was wary about missing anything because she wasn't concentrating, and their voices would carry over the barren landscape. She missed listening to Zamira's lilting voice, but that was even more reason to stay quiet. Distraction could be deadly.

They arrived at the location Flick had identified in her plan as a reasonable overnight spot, and she was pleased that it was as good as she'd hoped. Sitting in her office looking at maps and aerial photographs with Alex was completely different to being on the ground. She'd done this many times and had gotten it wrong twenty percent of the time when the maps and photos had been too old and had missed new buildings, or they'd been inaccurate and put the location in the wrong place. But luck was on her side, and with so many possible enemies, she wanted their last night in Tarinor to be trouble free.

The boulder against her back made it ache, but that helped keep her awake as dawn slowly approached. Zamira curled up against her. Her breathing was light and regular, and the warmth of her body was comforting. Flick was more than a little concerned about the day ahead. Her plan involved them being Lyulli who didn't recognize borders and crossed wherever they pleased to get wherever they were going. Their families had traveled these routes for generations. The border checkpoints wouldn't stop them if they fell for it. But they'd be on the lookout for Zamira and would recognize her if they looked closely. In which case, they'd end up in a firefight. The Pakistan border police probably wouldn't get involved. It was just what was waiting for them on this side of the border that worried her. She missed Chalky and Slim, with their extra armaments and experience. Getting through the border would have been much easier. Her adrenaline was working overtime, and while it gave her extra energy and clarity of thought and vision, it also filled her mind with thoughts that she'd rather leave buried.

She hadn't spent time with any woman since Leah and lying with her arms around Zamira had made her revisit her feelings of loss. They always say that grief will pass after traveling through a number of stages. She never knew what those stages were but looking back, she knew she'd been through a number of them. When Leah had first passed, she'd refused to accept she was dead, and when she realized she wasn't coming back, she'd raged at the world, at the Army, the Navy, and the government for putting her in the position that she'd been killed. Leah wasn't a combatant. She didn't have a gun, and although she'd used one in training, she'd never fired one in anger. But arguably, her job of providing intel was as much on the front line as if she had a weapon. Her softness and lack of anger ensured Flick would never think of her as a fighter. Flick was still alive and continuing to fight, but God or whoever it was in charge of cutting people's strings down here should have taken her instead. She was the person with the hardness inside that enabled her to do this job and be good at it. Leah wasn't. She should've been saved. Flick would have given anything to have taken her place.

The worst thing for her as she lay there on a mountain in Tarinor in the darkness and in another woman's arms was the searing pain that still tainted her blood. The sort of pain that took her breath away. *I still think about you every day. I don't know how I'm supposed to keep going without you.*

Now she had another woman in her arms, and they fit together well, although they were completely different. She wasn't certain she knew what to think about it. The hint of attraction bothered her, and guilt rose like bile.

Light was just beginning to chase away the darkness when she awoke Zamira by giving her a gentle rub on her arm. Flick leaned in close. "We need to be on the move. Let's have some water and go over the plans for today."

Zamira took a few moments to wake up. Flick wondered how anyone could look so beautiful having spent the night asleep on the ground in the ice cold of the mountain. She pushed the thought aside. This wasn't the time or place and dammed if she'd cheat on Leah's memory.

She handed Zamira her gun. "I'll just remind you how it works. I know you don't want to use it, and I understand," Flick said. "But if it comes down to them or us, and you want to live to see freedom, you may not have a choice."

Zamira stared at the ground before looking at Flick. "I don't think I'll ever be able to use it at all. But I'll do as you say, in case," she said.

Grateful that Zamira had stopped fighting her, she reminded her about how it worked and loaded a full cartridge of ammo. Zamira put the gun in the waistband of her trousers, and they set out. They were high above the pass, and the track was both uneven and treacherous in the half-light, but it took them swiftly downwards. As they headed down, Flick could hear her heart beating. She was sweating despite the cold.

The light rose in the distance, and as they came closer to ground level of the pass, she saw the checkpoint in the distance. They came to a road that joined the pass after they went up the goat track. Flick had planned it so that they had the minimum time on or near the road. The lights went off as the sun came over the horizon, and Flick lengthened her stride, wanting to get there before shift change.

"Come along, my Lyulli brother, let's get going." She said it loudly enough to be overheard by anyone lurking in the shadows. "Be ready to draw your gun and use it, either before or at the checkpoint," she whispered.

It was just as she expected. The sky was grayish, and there were still nightly shadows in places. The bad light would be helpful. The area between the road and the checkpoint was flat, the once asphalted road full of gravel and rock fillings that were often not level with the road. Some areas rose and fell like a tray of badly made cakes. Flick subtly looked around and walked slowly. She had her arm around Zamira. The Tarin checkpoint was a series of red and white concrete blocks placed across the road with metal poles between them to allow only one vehicle through at a time. The barrier was unmanned.

Set off to the side between them and the barrier was the Tarinor Border Control Office. The single-story building was constructed from local rock and cement and had a flat roof. There were no windows that Flick could see, although she expected the front of the building to have a window. As they drew closer, the stench of men living miles from habitation and proper sanitary conditions became apparent. The smell of raw sewage and rotting food permeated the air, making her stomach turn.

As they neared the front of the building, Flick gripped Zamira tightly. "The next five minutes will decide if we live or die. Get ready to act as if your life depended on it, and if our act fails, run. Shoot if you can or need to."

A border guard sat on the front porch, drinking from a cup. He didn't wear a cap, and his hair was thinning. He was an older man who didn't look particularly fit, and his guard's outfit hung on his thin frame.

He tilted upright in his chair and motioned at them. "We have to check everyone leaving the country. A woman has escaped prison, and they think she may try to cross the border here," he said. "Come over here and let me check your papers, if you have them."

Flick turned toward him with their papers in her hand. "We're headed over to visit family in Pamelbak, like we did a few months ago. You didn't stop us then," she said.

The guard stood and threw the remains of his drink onto the ground in front of him. "I haven't worried up till now, but there's two men here who insist I check everyone," he said, pointing to the room behind him.

He held out their papers to the men they couldn't see. Flick didn't like it. A little of Chalky's explosive would have been the perfect thing to provide a distraction. The border was so close and yet so far away. It looked as if it was probably going to be a shootout, there was no way around it. She took a deep breath to prepare herself. She put her hand on to her gun, ready to move.

She lifted her chin and listened to the familiar rushing in her ears and the tingling of adrenaline as she became totally alert. All her training and experience kicked in. She took in the whole scene at a glance and spotted a man as he appeared in the doorway dressed in jeans and a leather jacket. Her senses were so alert, she could describe his moustache, small and thick; his sunglasses, Lexxola Jordy's; and the handgun, a Smith & Wesson M&P he was now pointing at them.

Zamira bent her head slightly toward Flick. "Man from the plane," she mouthed.

This was it. They'd run out of time and luck.

Flick didn't hesitate. She took out her gun and shot the man standing in the doorway in the middle of his forehead as he aimed at them. He fell forward with a look of surprise still on his face. The border guard froze.

Flick grabbed Zamira and pushed her. "Run as fast as you can. Don't stop for anything," she said. She'd have to do a fifty-yard dash to get to the Pakistan border barrier and a further fifty yards to get under cover. But the fear of capture and death were good motivators.

Flick ducked behind one of the concrete border posts as a figure appeared inside the darkened border post doorway and started firing at her. She wasn't quick enough to get out of the way and pain blossomed keen and sharp in her shoulder. She cursed herself for getting unfit working a desk. She'd been shot before but never in her shoulder, and it felt like it might have gone all the way through. Two wounds, one in back, one in front. How fast would she grow dizzy from loss of blood?

She looked around the post and took in the scene once more as if the whole situation was in slow motion. The border guard was still struggling to get his gun out of the pouch on his belt, his face a picture of concentration as he wiped sweat from his eyes. She had a moment to focus on the man who had shot her. He was probably another of the presidential guards and a professional. He was clever and stayed in the shadow of the doorway. She was lit up as if under a spotlight in the rising sun, and she had to keep the attention on herself to allow Zamira to get away and out of range.

She emptied her clip into the dark of the doorway and waited. The moments following passed slowly, and every sound magnified. Loud footsteps took her attention. The border guard had found his courage and had run forward, his arms extended, and his gun pointed at her head. He was about to shoot her. Flick had been following his movements, worried he was going after Zamira, and she was already turning when she heard a gun discharge from behind her and the border guard grabbed his stomach and fell forward.

"Zamira?"

Zamira was behind her, open-mouthed and stumbling forward, the gun still in her outstretched hands.

Flick turned and pulled her down behind the concrete. "You're supposed to be safe in Pakistan," she said.

"I was...was going... I thought he was coming for you. I couldn't let him." Zamira retched.

Flick took her gun from Zamira's hands. She wanted to put her arms around her and tell her everything was going to be okay. She'd never had that reaction to any of the women she'd rescued over the years. But this wasn't the time. Shock was about to overcome Zamira, and they had to get over the border.

Flick took stock and surveyed the scene. There was no movement from the doorway of the building. The gunman with the moustache hadn't moved. The border guard was still. Flick wondered if there was yet another border guard, since it was unusual for there to be just one. She put another magazine in her gun. Her shoulder hurt like hell, and her neck and upper body were on fire.

She held Zamira's gun in her left hand. It wouldn't be useful at hitting the mark, but it would get close and help provide cover. "We're going to run together. If I stop to fire my weapons, keep going. If you can't do that, then stand behind me," Flick said. She stood, pulling Zamira up with her, and waited for a shot to sound. Flick closed her eyes. *One, two, three.*

They turned and ran.

Shots fired, and the air around them cracked and shattered under bullets slamming into the ground. There was another border guard, or the presidential guard was still alive. Perhaps both. Flick turned and saw a shadow in the window of the building firing at them. She let loose a few rounds from her good hand and glass shattered. Even if she hadn't managed to get the shooter, he would've had to take cover. She'd felt Zamira right behind her. They turned and ran and kept running, bullets following, until they were in the border control building in Pakistan.

Inside was a high counter with a smart-looking uniformed guard behind it. "You Lyulli. Sometimes the border guards have a bit of sport at your expense. Looks like you drew the short straw. You have anything they may want in your bags?"

Flick handed them both over the counter without saying a word.

The Pakistani guard looked at the meager contents of the bags and laughed. "A little food, water, and some ammo. Not worth their trouble."

Flick was a little unsteady on her feet and leaned against the counter. "We'll be on our way," she said. "By treating Lyulli men and women like this, they have no honor. They call us trash and the lowest form of life, and they would happily kill us without a second thought." Continuing with the charade would buy them time if anyone came over asking about them or demanding their capture. Flick had to get them through the little village near the checkpoint without letting anyone on the Tarin side get a look at them through a sniper rifle. She nodded to the Pakistani guard and looked back at the border crossing. She couldn't see anything unusual, but that didn't mean anything. There was still at least one person over there alive enough to shoot. And they knew what disguises she and Zamira were traveling in. But they only had to survive here a little while longer. She swayed a little. No problem.

CHAPTER ELEVEN

Z AMIRA COULDN'T SEE MORE than a few steps in front of her. It was damaged tarmac, potholes, rock, and dust. She concentrated on the roadway and looked at the pockmarked surface. She dared not think of anything else. Her insides were wooden, and she was sure that if she moved her head too quickly, she would be sick. She'd used Flick's gun, and she'd taken a life. *No, don't think about it. Just keep your mind on the potholes.*

"We're leaving the road here and heading cross country," Flick said. "We need to get to our pickup point. It's about a day's walk away if we're lucky."

She couldn't bring herself to talk, so she just nodded. Zamira changed her focus. The dusty potholes were now clumps of yellow-brown grass. It was difficult to walk across, but it had been the same for the whole journey. *Just remember walking across the plain and do the same now. Put one foot in front of the other. I can do this. We're nearly there.*

"The Tarin authorities will be after us soon. We may have left a border guard alive at the checkpoint, and he'll have gotten in touch with his bosses. They'll be over the border before we can get far. The stream will give us plenty of cover, and it goes cross country almost to our RV. You need to stay alert in case they follow us. I don't think they're allowed to use choppers in this area, but they may not care much about permission," Flick said.

Zamira nodded again. She hung onto Flick's arm and moved forward one step at a time. How could she have used that gun?

The border guard was going to shoot Flick. But she might have been able to shoot him first. Zamira had been frightened Flick would die, and she was her only way to escape. Flick was important to her, but how was that possible after so little time together? She was awkward and rude. If she hadn't taught her to use a gun, Zamira wouldn't be in this position. Thoughts went around and around her mind, and tears slid unheeded down her cheeks.

It was only when Flick stumbled and went down on one knee that Zamira really looked at her. The bloodstain on her shoulder was too big, too dark. "You've been shot?" Zamira knelt next to her. "I didn't know." She reached out, her hand hovering over the spot, but she didn't know what to do. She trembled from deep inside.

"The bullet went all the way through if you can see blood on the back of my shirt. That's a good thing. I'll fix it up when we're farther away." Flick struggled back to her feet. "Come on."

They walked for a while before resting briefly to take a drink of water. Zamira sat on a rock. "You'd better take your clothes off again so that we can look at your wound. Once we can see what's happened, we can work out what we need to do," she said.

Flick looked pale and moved gingerly.

Zamira stood and moved in front of her. "Let me do this. You're obviously in pain and only have one good arm." She lifted the bags from Flick's other shoulder, and Flick put her hand out as if to stop her. Zamira readied a retort but Flick merely nodded.

"Thank you. It's not as if you haven't seen me naked yet," she said.

She smiled and tried to help as Zamira started taking her top layers off. The wound at the front looked relatively small. Zamira had expected to see a round bullet hole the size of a penny. Instead, it was only a few millimeters across. There was only a little blood. "It's only a small hole at the front," Zamira said.

"It may be small, but it hurts like hell. Right the way through to the other side," Flick said, dipping her chin to see into the wound and then looking over her shoulder to get a glimpse of the exit wound.

"Is there anything in this bit of shoulder that the bullet might have hit?" Zamira asked. "I don't know the human body in that much detail."

"Arteries, and nerves, and bones if I'm unlucky. But I can't see a lot of blood. I can still feel my arm and hand, and I didn't hear a bone crack when the bullet went in. What does the exit wound look like?" Flick asked.

"It's bigger. Not that much, but it has more blood and is much redder. What do we do with it?" Zamira asked.

"Use the cleanest cloth we have to cover both wounds and then strap it up tight. We should keep it dry and make sure we don't get anything more into it." She looked at her shirt in Zamira's hands and then at Zamira. "Is my shirt sleeve the cleanest we have?"

"Yes, I think so, and you know where it came from. Mine came from the Lyulli and may not have been clean to start with," Zamira said.

Flick used her teeth to tear the shirt sleeve off, and Zamira tore it in two. She put one piece over the exit wound and then used Flick's breast band to hold it in place before doing similarly to the front. Flick winced each time Zamira covered the wounds and when she tightened the strap. But she didn't make a sound. Zamira felt certain she wouldn't have been as stoic if it had been her. "Your arm may get tired and ache. I think you should use one of your shoulder bags as a sling. We can put everything in the other bag, and I'll carry it," Zamira said.

Flick nodded, looking tired and pale. "As long as we keep moving."

Zamira helped Flick dress, picked up the other bag, and they set off again.

They didn't speak. Zamira still seethed at having to use the gun. She didn't want it to have happened, and she didn't want to have these feelings of anger. She'd never lose the feeling of loss that the shooting had given her. The loss of a life wasn't inconsequential, no matter the circumstances. It was going to stay with her, be her unwanted partner for the rest of her life.

Flick was different. She had gotten used to it. She'd said in an unguarded moment on the plain that she'd shot a few people, and it didn't get any easier, that she would take all those shots through life with her, and she had to accept that was who she was and what she'd done. If she couldn't deal with the weight of those lives, perhaps she should consider getting out and doing something which didn't involve her killing people.

Zamira had been amazed that Flick had the mental strength to rescue her despite losing her two best friends hours before they met. Zamira didn't have that strength of purpose. She looked at Flick, marching silently ahead and often scanning the area around them. When her helicopter crashed, she could have left. She could've decided it wasn't worth the risk. But here she was, wounded and still determined to get Zamira to safety. She brushed away tears. How had things gotten so bad? She just wanted her life back.

It was late afternoon when Flick finally called a halt.

"We should stay here overnight. There's good cover and water. But before we do anything else, we should talk about the checkpoint and what happened there," she said.

"Talk about what happened? Talk about me shooting that guard, don't you mean?" Zamira felt heat rise from her neck. Her anger inside was like a pressure cooker with the lid firmly on. Once released, it blew like a steam vent. "You don't get it. It's all your fault. If you hadn't taught me how to use a gun, I wouldn't have shot that man," she said.

Flick stood in front of her. "Zamira, if you hadn't shot him, I could be dead. Thank you."

"It's still your fault. You made me learn to use it. I don't want to feel like this. I'm a murderer, and I don't want to be one. I can't take it back. It's all down to you." She pushed at Flick's chest, lashing out at the person who had armed her. "I should have just run across the checkpoint like you said and left you there."

Flick grabbed Zamira's arm with her good hand. "Why didn't you?"

Yes. Why didn't she? She stopped in her tracks. She deflated, her rage flattened by the question. Flick was right. She'd had the means to get clear and free and yet, she'd stayed. She wouldn't leave her rescuer behind. She wouldn't leave someone she cared about.

Zamira looked up into Flick's shadowed eyes and was transfixed. Flick bent her head slowly toward her. Her lips were a breath away, and she was still entranced by the intensity in her eyes. Zamira said nothing as Flick kissed her gently. The kiss lasted a moment that could have been five seconds or five minutes. Either way, it was a bag full of contrasting adjectives. It was unexpected but at the same time, planned. It was exciting and at the same time, felt like a warm hug. It was amazing and at the same time, it could have been nothing out of the ordinary. Her tummy fluttered. Her racing heartbeat was surely broadcasting out over the hills.

Zamira had no idea what she'd been saying a moment before. This was just too much to cope with on top of everything. She hadn't realized she might have some feelings for Flick. Or she hadn't wanted to acknowledge them. She couldn't think straight and therefore said nothing. She enjoyed the moment in Flick's arms, surrounded by warmth and her eyes watching her every expression.

"Mm. That was delicious. Maybe we can do it again," Flick said.

Zamira nodded her head slowly, and their lips touched for the second time. This time, Zamira took notice of all the things she'd missed the first time around. Flick's lips were warm and soft against hers, despite the cool air. When she moved her tongue over her lips, Zamira almost sighed. The second kiss was longer than the first and filled with tension and promise. But a promise of what?

Flick took a step back. "Let's find somewhere to camp. We're both worn out, and I need to rest my shoulder."

Zamira looked around at the gully they'd stopped in. The stream was some twenty feet below the surrounding land and had rocks of different sizes all along it. She led Flick along the stream until she found a flat area they could settle in. The abundance of rocks would hide them well from any casual observer.

"I'm impressed," Flick said as she slumped to the ground. "I need to get a bit more pressure on my back, and this rock will be ideal. It's flat too. You're good at this. Maybe you should join my department." She gave Zamira a wry grin and then closed her eyes.

Zamira knelt beside her and took the stove out of the bag along with a bottle of water. "I've had a good teacher. I'll make us some tea. I can get fresh water for tomorrow later."

"There's still some goat left from last night," Flick said.

They'd both decided that the liquid wasn't brilliant without any herbs or salt. They'd eaten it with the broth but decided to keep just the meat. It was tender, and there had been plenty of it. Zamira wasn't exactly starving, but she could eat a whole loaf of bread without stopping and totally ignore the goat. "I'm still hankering after a pizza though," she said.

Flick laughed. "You'll be able get one within forty-eight hours," she said. "After we eat, I'll tell you the plan for tomorrow, so you have a good idea of what's going to happen."

Zamira couldn't help but sit back and enjoy their friendly chat. They'd spent most of the time they'd been together annoyed or cross with each other. Well, if she were honest, she was the one who'd instigated most of it. She'd called Flick incompetent when she'd managed to get Zamira out of the prison and to safety, even though she was on her own after her team were killed. Then there was the gun issue. Suddenly, she was back at the checkpoint. Flick was in danger from that guard. He was running toward her holding his gun out in front of him. Flick would have been killed.

Zamira closed her eyes, reliving the moment. Part of her was still angry at having to use the gun, but with a little time and distance, she'd realized that it had been necessary. Zamira would have been on her own, trying to survive without a guide, running from the people who wanted to hurt her, hurt her father. It had to be done. Unbidden, a sob escaped. Was this her life now?

When she opened her eyes, Flick had gotten up and was kneeling in front of her, holding her hand. She was obviously in a lot of discomfort. Her face was pale, her expression worried.

"You're all right, my sweet girl. You're safe. We're still sitting by the stream, and you're making tea. Although I'll die of thirst at this rate." Flick smiled.

"I suddenly thought..." Zamira wasn't sure she could talk about it. She pushed down her worries. She needed to be less of a pain from now on.

Flick didn't move. "I'm hoping you feel safe with me and know that we can talk about anything. I've shared more with you about my life and feelings than I've ever shared with anyone other than Leah. It's been good to talk about things with you. You're a good listener. I know you're angry." Flick sighed, stood up, and began to pace. "I can't take that anger away. But I do understand it. The situation here is one of survival, and when your life is on the line, things change. To survive, you have to do things you don't want to, things you would never usually do." She turned and faced Zamira. "I've been trained to this life. But I've rescued women from situations where they've done *anything* to survive, used their bodies, taken drugs, and killed if they had to. I'm not saying your life is like theirs, but it isn't too different. You've been lucky till now." She fell silent for a moment. "You've done brilliantly, and we're almost home. You've survived. Can you tell me what you were thinking just then?" Flick asked.

"I can, but I worry that talking about it will give it substance. I want it to go away, not become more concrete," Zamira said.

"I've always believed that talking about it takes the sharp, agonizing pain out of it. Trust me. It makes any memory purely something that happened, but not something that's going to ruin your life," Flick said. "If you hold it in, it becomes a growth, a black spot on your soul that can spread."

"I do trust you," Zamira said and realized it was true. Somehow over the last four days, she had come to trust Flick. "I was making the tea and before I knew it, I was reliving the checkpoint and not wanting to shoot the gun. My past ideas about not taking a life seem illogical. Because when I was behind the barrier and in the moment, I didn't think. I didn't hesitate.

I just shot him." She leaned toward Flick, wanting her closeness and the feeling of safety that she gave. "I was going to an academic conference in Japan to talk about government corruption, and suddenly I'm in prison. Then I'm fighting for my life on the high plains and being shot at on the border. I keep asking myself, why me?" Tears ran down her face as she tried to control her feelings.

"Let it all go. Let all those tears out. Thinking about the 'Why me?' scenario will do you no good, believe me. When Leah was first killed, I yelled at the unfairness and shouted, 'Why her?' from the rooftops. Between that and 'Why not me?' I was in free fall. It's a deep chasm to fall into and takes a long time to get out of," Flick said.

Zamira understood. She'd been screaming similar things when her mumma died. She was the only one of her friends without a mother, and she didn't understand why she'd had to leave her. The loss had almost unhinged her. Perhaps she'd be able to look at things differently in the weeks to come, once the rawness had lessened a little.

"I'll work on it," Zamira said. She took the water bottle out of the bag and poured it into their cooking pan. She split the tea into two, so there'd be enough for the morning. They sat in silence for a while, and she looked at Flick. "Can I ask you something personal?"

Flick's eyebrow rose, and she nodded.

"Who are you? In regular life."

Flick frowned and stared at the ground. "That's a strange question. What do you mean?"

"You've told me a little about your family. I'm guessing there's plenty more. You speak multiple languages, but you don't say anything much about yourself, about the true you. Is it hard? To lie about who you are all the time?"

"Wow." Flick leaned back. "That sounds harsh, but I guess there's some truth to it. No, it isn't hard. Not when I'm doing good work. Those lies can help keep the people in my life safe."

Zamira tilted her head as she stared at the sky. "I would find it hard. Impossible, I think, to never really be known or understood."

"Good thing you're not in my line of work then." Flick took the water bottles to the stream to refill them and added water purifying tablets while the tea water boiled on the stove. "We just need this stove to last one more day. Tomorrow would be difficult without a cup of tea." She pulled the package of goat meat toward her and started to split it into two portions. "Do you want your meat first? I think I'll have mine now and wash it down with the tea," she said.

"Wise words, my friend. I'll do the same," Zamira said.

Flick handed her a parcel of meat. "Do you mean that?" she said.

There was a soft rawness to her tone that made Zamira look over. "That you're my friend? Yes, I do." Zamira moved closer to her. "You're perhaps more than a friend, but I don't want to give you a label yet. Another kiss will work that out." Zamira dropped to her knees and leaned over. "Don't move. I don't want you in any more pain."

"You're very bossy," Flick said and grinned.

Zamira placed her lips against Flick's, and there was the familiar thrum in her stomach and the beat of her heart. They both stank. They were both filthy. But in this moment, nothing mattered but getting to kiss Flick once again.

Zamira continued exploring, enjoying the taste and the feeling the kiss gave her. She wanted more but wasn't sure this was the time or place. Flick seemed to be in a lot of pain. She pulled away, gently smiling at the look of disappointment in Flick's eyes. She packed their things away in case they had to make a quick exit during the night. The sun disappeared as she finished her tea.

Flick lay down but gave a sudden intake of breath.

"Will it be better to lay on your back?" Zamira asked. "I can curl up to you on the other side to your wound. It'll help keep you warm."

Flick grimaced. "I'll try it. If not, I'll sleep sitting up," she said. She moved around on the ground and eventually stilled. "I think this might be better than sitting. My back and neck muscles are relaxing a little."

Zamira put her blanket over Flick and then Flick's on top of that. "That should help keep the heat in," she said and wrapped herself around Flick's side. She leaned on her elbow and looked at Flick in the half-light. She should let her sleep. But her body was on fire, and she was desperate to touch Flick some more. "Could I kiss you again?"

Flick laughed. "I'm at your mercy," she said. "I don't want to move my arm, and you're lying on the other one."

Zamira could taste the tea on Flick's lips as she continued her exploration. She'd never had the chance to go wherever she wanted on a woman's body, and she could hear her own heart beating and feel Flick's heart pounding against her breast.

She moved her body over Flick's as she nibbled gently at her ear. Flick breathed deeply. "Are you in pain?" Zamira asked.

Flick's breath stuttered. "Yes, but not from the bullet wound. It's the pain of feeling your breasts against my body and not being able to do a thing about it."

Zamira continued her heady journey, burying her lips into Flick's neck as she kissed and sucked. Flick held her close, her face pressed to her hair.

"I hurt," Flick said and let go of her. "I don't want to stop. I want to be close to you. But it's no good, I can't. I'm sorry."

Zamira moved her weight off Flick. "How can I help?"

"Perhaps you could just sit up. I need to move around a little." Flick changed position. "Ah, yes, that's it... Come back and just... Yes, perfect."

Zamira replaced the blankets, lay down with her head on Flick's shoulder and cuddled up to her. She'd never been so close to anyone before. It was as if it was meant to be. Tomorrow, if all went well, it would be over. She would go back to being an academic, and Flick would go back to being a rescuer of women like her. Had Flick had romantic interludes with the other women she'd rescued? The thought made her shift uncomfortably. It was none of her business. But allowing her heart to get involved would be foolish. She held Flick tightly, knowing the opportunity to do so would soon come to an end.

CHAPTER TWELVE

AT LAST. FLICK WATCHED the sun rise, grateful that a new day had begun. The night had been long and painful. Her shoulder had ached, and the pain had spread over her arm, side, and neck. She tried not to grit her teeth and increase the tension. She used some meditation techniques, but her concentration was off. A mixture of pain, worry that the helo pickup might not work, and an undercurrent of lust kept her fidgeting and disturbing Zamira. Although Zamira made light of it every time she woke her up, Flick suspected that she'd had little sleep too. She thought back to those mornings when they had been cuddled together to keep warm in the ice-cold winds of the high plain, and she'd awoken with Zamira's hair in her face. She wished she could have that on this, their last morning, but it was now just a memory.

There were few positions that helped with the pain now. She needed medical attention as soon as possible. Zamira was still sound asleep. Flick pushed a ruck of blanket under her head and moved to lean against a rock. She looked down at Zamira as she slept and watched a strand of her hair move each time Zamira breathed out. Flick remembered the previous evening and the warmth and kisses they'd shared. That first kiss had been a surprise. Flick had no idea she was going to kiss Zamira. Then Zamira had kissed her back, an even bigger surprise.

She had feelings for Zamira, but what was the point? They lived very different lives. And in the light of the morning, guilt about Leah wrapped around like barbed wire. She should move on now. It was time. But there were still threads that she hadn't let go of. She and Leah had been joined in so many ways, and Flick had to cut those last strings. That didn't mean that she should pursue Zamira. It was unprofessional to sleep with a rescue. It could result in her being unfocused and unable to separate her emotions from the job. But Zamira no longer felt like just a job. She was feisty, tender, caring, and intelligent. She brought out every protective instinct Flick had. Was there any future for them?

Zamira's feelings were a whole other kettle of fish to examine. She could just be grateful. She could be confusing gratitude for attraction. They'd spent a few days together in a high stress atmosphere, with attempts on their lives and being chased across Tarinor. Their feelings were bound to be tied together, though it had never happened before. And Flick had rescued her. It probably wasn't the sort of start a relationship should have. She couldn't work out how they'd manage a life together. They were just so different. Their backgrounds and upbringing, their formative years, their careers, and even where they lived. But they had a connection and had it all been different, she might have followed up on it. But things were what they were, and when they left each other later today, she would say goodbye and leave it at that.

"Hey," Zamira said. Her voice was about an octave lower than usual. "Could you pass me some of that water, please? And tell me you weren't sitting watching me with my mouth wide open and some terrible noise coming out."

Flick passed her the water bottle. "I was a little worried that bears might come around looking for one of their own, but–" She grinned and ducked the pebble Zamira threw at her. Keeping things light would make it easier to say goodbye later.

Zamira sat up and downed half the bottle. "How are you feeling?" she asked.

"If I'm honest, I'll be pleased to get back to civilization. I need pain killers and antibiotics, and I'll have to have the whole wound flushed before it's stitched." She grimaced and sighed. "Once we've had our tea, we need to get moving. I'd like to be at our RV by midday. Help should be with us soon after that."

"After we've used the water for tea, I'll fill our water bottles. While I'm gone, I'll use the latrine, as you call it. I'll be quick and careful, promise," Zamira said as she tipped water into their pan.

As they drank their tea, Flick gave Zamira the details of the phone call she had to make and what she would be saying, as well as what to expect after. If anything else happened to them and Flick didn't make it, Zamira could manage the escape on her own. The pickup point was close to the site of a fallen down shepherd's hut, with only the remnants of the rock walls left. The walls would provide a good hiding place and shelter while they waited. The helo would land a short distance away, and they had to be there at the agreed time. Flick was only too aware of the dangers of trying to fly a helo in this area. There were several possible expected pickup points in the plan, although her department would be targeting the signal on her burner phone.

Zamira packed up their belongings and put the bag over her shoulder. She didn't draw attention to it, and Flick was pleased not to have to discuss it. She couldn't carry it, but she wasn't one to stand by and watch a woman struggle with bags, be they shopping, suitcases, or in this case, their worldly goods. At least this way, her good hand was free to use a weapon if it came to that again.

They walked along the side of the stream for about five miles when Flick halted them. "By my calculations, the pickup point is close by, so let's look up over the lip of the gully. It should be over there." Flick pointed toward the nearby hill. She scrambled up the side of the gully, feeling every painful step. Her previous wounds had been nothing as bad as this. Looking over the edge, she was conscious of Zamira moving up close alongside her.

"I've seen you move better than that. You're really hurting, aren't you?" Zamira asked.

Flick nodded, not daring to speak. Admitting weakness to the person you were rescuing wasn't a good look.

Zamira patted her hand. "There's a pile of rocks over there. Is that the sort of thing we should be looking for?"

"That's not the RV point. It's too close to the gully. But I expect if we move to those rocks, we'll be able to see the RV point. The next few minutes are when we're going to be most exposed, so we need to be aware. I need your sharp eyes and ears. Like before, point out anything out of the ordinary," Flick said.

"Okay. I think we should have a ten-minute rest and some water before we go. You need to drink something," Zamira said.

Flick turned slowly and slid down the bank. She stayed where she landed, lying on her back with her eyes closed. It felt good and was temporary relief from the pain. The sun was warm on her face, and her skin warmed through her clothes.

"Drink," Zamira said, passing her a water bottle.

Flick sat up and took it. Once she'd had a drink, she stood. "Let's get on with it, shall we?" She scrambled up the gully bank for the second time and looked out over the top before moving forward. The ground ahead was covered with the brown and yellow grass that they'd crossed on much of their journey. Rocks continued to litter their way and make the going rough. Flick had to concentrate and was looking at her feet and counting her footsteps to keep herself going. Her energy was flagging, and her skin was hot to the touch. Infection was setting in. She had to finish this mission and fast. They reached the pile of rocks they'd seen from the gully quickly, and Flick could see the hut's broken walls up ahead. There was no one around as far as she could see.

Once they'd reached the broken hut, Flick took out the burner phone and dialed a number.

"Yes?"

"This is Kingfisher. Two PAX, loc one," she said.

"Yes."

The phone went dead. "Now we wait. I expect it'll be an hour," Flick said. "I might close my eyes for a moment, just to rest. Will you keep watch?"

Zamira nodded. "Do you want more water? You're looking pale. I want to give you something to make you feel better, but we only have water."

She smiled and her face lit up. Her lips turned up at the corners, her eyes brightened, and Flick wished she'd spent more time trying to make her laugh instead of making her angry or cry.

"What are you thinking?" Zamira asked. "I caught a wistful look."

She didn't have the energy to keep things hidden. "I was regretting not making you smile much in our time together. I love seeing it, however momentary."

"You do?"

Flick couldn't hang onto the conversation any longer. She closed her eyes and drifted away. She became aware of the sound of a chopper's thrum getting louder. She opened her eyes and the excitement burst through her. The journey was nearly over. She struggled to stand, and Zamira helped her to her feet. "We need to walk over there, and the helo will come to us," Flick said. "When we get there, kneel so you make a small target, and keep clear of the rotors. Someone on the chopper will signal what they want you to do."

Flick led the way to the point she'd indicated, and they both knelt. In the couple of minutes walking across the grass, the helo closed in, and Flick started thinking about being shot out of the sky. She recalled the freefall through the air, the explosions, and the burning. Nausea rose, and she dry retched. There was nothing much in her stomach to come up. Zamira went into her bag to get water, but Flick shook her head. She didn't want a bottle to get swept into the engine. She had to stop thinking this way. The flight would be fine and would take her one step nearer to home.

A woman on the helo gestured them forward and helped Zamira on-board. Flick pointed to her shoulder and shouted, "Injured." She recognized Mary from her department. She nodded and put out her hand. Flick grabbed it as she jumped and was simultaneously pulled in with a steel-like grip. She was on board before she could worry about the resulting pain. She and Zamira settled on the floor in the dark and tomb-like area behind the pilots that normally carried troops. Two men wearing jeans, T-shirts, and leather jackets were carrying heavy machine guns looking out of the doors. The helo took off.

Mary leaned toward Flick and shouted into her ear. "Hi, Flick. What injury do you have? Do you need a medic?"

"GSW to the shoulder, in and out. Yes to the medic. Infection likely," Flick said.

Mary stood and leaned over to the pilot. When she turned she gave a thumbs-up. Then she ducked. "SHIT!"

Bullets slammed into the helo like dried peas being shot onto a tin roof with a catapult. The two men fired into the mountainside. The helo dipped and rose, tilted and turned. Sweat flooded down Flick's back, and her heart felt like it would explode.

As quickly as the firing had started, it was over. The helo gained height, and they were away. Flick saw holes some of the shots had made. The men slid the doors closed, and darkness took over.

Zamira sat next to her, wide-eyed and pale. It was no good trying to say anything more than a few words to her over the noise of the engines and the air rushing into the space. She nudged her hand and gestured to ask if she was all right. Zamira nodded. Flick wasn't convinced. She held her hand and closed her eyes.

Over the thrum of the engines, Flick thought about the people who had lost their lives during the mission. Chalky and Slim were two of the people that knew both her and Leah well, and their loss was going to be another wound in her soul. Leah, Chalky, Slim. How many more people could she lose? She was toxic to her friends. She had asked them to do something, and they had died. She couldn't keep on doing this. She wasn't strong enough.

Her eyes welled up, and she had trouble seeing clearly. She took her hand from Zamira and wiped the tears that had started falling down her cheeks. She was going to have to restart her life again. Her head was muzzy from the effects of the wound, and her kaleidoscope of thoughts made the pain worse. Visiting Chalky and Slim's families would be hell, but she owed it to them. Maybe she'd try to find the pilot's family. Memories of Leah laughing with her when they watched some old black and white movies of the Keystone cops flooded her mind. Then Zamira angry and shouting at her on the high plains. The pain in her shoulder was so bad, she could see it in her mind. The picture was like one of those posters of a small black hole in the universe with a red crust around the edge, and a spaceship firing nuclear missiles into it, over and over. The pain from the missiles was acute but in the gaps between the missiles, the pain abated briefly before it hit her again.

The helo landed, the loud heavy engine noise slowly reduced, and Mary opened one of the doors. The darkness of the tomb was replaced by bright sunlight. Flick stood, pulled Zamira up, and led her to the door. Zamira jumped down onto the ground, but Flick couldn't do it. Dizzy and weak, she slid to the floor using her good arm to hold her against the edge of the door until she sat with her legs hanging from the helo deck.

There was little that Flick could see of the airfield except a medical team with a stretcher. It was all in her peripheral vision as she watched Zamira looking around her. Flick was paralyzed. This was the moment she needed to do something or *say* something that would bridge the sudden chasm between them. They would be taken into medical and debriefing, and she may not get a chance to have much of a private conversation again. Her heart beat loudly, and she felt sick, but no words would come.

She couldn't believe it had come to this. She had a vocabulary of thousands of words in many languages, but she couldn't say anything at all. Flick wanted Zamira to stay and work out whatever was between them, to find out whether it was nothing but smoke and mirrors.

Zamira turned and looked at her. The air was heavy with expectation and questions.

Zamira stepped back. "There's nothing for me with you. We're so very different. You'll go back to your life and the lies you tell to live. You'll lie about what you do to the people in your daily life. You'll be the rescuer and lie about who you are to the people you carry away. You always live as someone else. I liked the real you I saw. Thank you for getting me out." She touched Flick's cheek gently. "Goodbye." She stretched onto her tiptoes and placed a soft kiss on Flick's cheek, turned, and walked away to follow Mary into the nearest building.

Flick sat as immobile as a statue. Zamira was completely correct. She *did* live a lie. She'd always lived as someone else for her job, and she'd loved doing it. But maybe she'd been doing it as part of living her life too.

Zamira headed off across the concrete and out of her life. Rescuing women from impossible situations was something she loved, and it was important to her. She had sat in her office, counting the moments as her life was passing her by. She'd needed to get out into the field again but now that she'd been there, she was unsure it was what she wanted. It had taken someone like Zamira to recognize that. Flick didn't know anymore. Losing people important to her had made her doubt herself, doubt what she wanted and cared about. She'd shown Zamira some of the real Flick, but that had left her not understanding what she should do next. She'd had to gloss over a lot about herself, because if they'd been captured, all that information could have been taken from Zamira and used against her, against her family.

Zamira had noticed. She sighed. Given the truth of a life that she wasn't happy with, it was hard to know how to change it. Her eyes misted up. Damn. She'd cried in the helo, and she was crying again now. She didn't cry. She was made of stronger stuff. Yet inside, she was screaming with anguish.

CHAPTER THIRTEEN

ZAMIRA HAD HOPED THAT Flick might say something when they were still at their campsite. Once she'd picked up their bags and they'd moved out, she'd waited for Flick to speak about where their shared kisses might take them. But she was silent. There was another opportunity as they walked together, as they waited for the helo, and finally, as they stood together at the airport. But Flick had said nothing at all. It was as though she'd already distanced herself and had said goodbye without a word.

Zamira had thought those kisses might have meant something. She'd ached with longing when they'd been lying together. She'd enjoyed their closeness and the fact that Flick was sharing their everyday decisions with her during the last couple of days. They'd shared thoughts, backgrounds, hopes, and fears. Zamira believed that they'd shared much more than a few kisses, and she'd hoped they could meet up once they went back to their lives.

But Flick had shut down. She'd closed off before they left their overnight camp. Zamira had thought that it was because she was in pain. Thinking back over it, she should have realized that Flick wouldn't want any more to do with her. She'd rescued her, completed the mission, and managed a short make-out session with the woman she'd saved. Now she would go back to her world. Zamira could have talked about it with Flick, she knew that. And yes, she'd put it all on Flick. But what should she say to someone who hadn't been straight with her for so much of the time they'd been together, someone who hadn't mentioned anything about the future. If Flick didn't talk about the future, how could Zamira?

She'd believed that Flick had feelings for her and would admit that, even if she didn't want to take things further. The silence had been damning. Zamira's anger grew by the minute. She wanted to scream, but she was stuck in this office waiting for some military stuffed-shirt to debrief her. She wasn't military and had little to say other than to tell her story. She hoped that would suffice.

The door opened and the woman from the helo came in. "Would you like a drink and some food?" she asked.

"Yes, please. We haven't eaten properly for days. I'm starving and would love anything vegetarian. Please don't offer me goat or rabbit," Zamira said and smiled a little at the thought of Flick trying to get her to eat meat.

"I'll bring you some toast to start with. Tea, coffee, or chocolate?"

Zamira could almost smell the hot chocolate. "Chocolate, please."

The woman was gone in an instant and returned with a small plate heaped with toast, some butter, and honey, and with a mug of hot chocolate. Zamira practically salivated over the small, simple meal.

"Please, help yourself," the woman said.

Before she could continue, Zamira grabbed the knife and spread butter and honey onto a hot slice of toast. She sat back and took a mouthful of heaven, and the woman smiled.

"I'll explain who I am and what we're doing while you eat. Once we finish, I'll sort out your flight home to Paris." She sat down opposite Zamira. "We've been recording this since you entered the room and will note what you say. This isn't because we think you've done anything wrong; it just enables us to revisit the facts as you see them and not miss something important. We may come back to you again if we find we need more information. Is your food okay?"

Zamira nodded. She lifted her mug and breathed in the chocolatey aroma.

"My name is Mary Grimes, and I work for the same department as Ms. Colonna. Call me Mary."

"You don't sound British, although I can't place your accent. And I expect your name isn't really Mary Grimes," Zamira said. *These people think I was born yesterday.* She was another one who didn't exist and if you looked too closely, would disappear. God only knew what Flick's real name was. The thought immediately bothered her. She'd been hoping to build a relationship with someone whose name she probably didn't even know. "You're all smoke and mirrors." Zamira sipped her chocolate, waiting for Mary to start her questions.

"Can we begin?" Mary asked.

Zamira had the impression she was a little frostier now.

"Tell me about what happened on the plane. I think that's a good starting point."

Zamira related the story as she'd lived it. She intentionally left out some things, like how she'd thought Flick was incompetent. She left out their fights about her not wanting to shoot a gun and not wanting to eat rabbit. She left out the kisses and the cuddles. She was an academic, and she'd been well trained and could therefore brief on the facts and her understanding of them, leaving out anything she deemed unnecessary. She showed Mary her necklace and bracelet which had given them access to the Tarinor Lyulli and explained how that had helped them escape Sayeb. The shooting at the checkpoint was her most difficult moment. She related the facts almost woodenly.

"Flick told you to run and leave her so that you could escape. Why didn't you?" Mary asked.

There was no way Zamira was going to tell her that she'd thought she had feelings for Flick. "I was turning to leave and saw the guard. He'd been trying to get his gun out of his holster and suddenly pulled it free. Flick was busy dealing with the men in the checkpoint office, and I thought the guard would kill either her or me," she said. "I knew I wouldn't get to safety without her." Far less emotional than the truth, but it would suffice.

"Were you expecting to use a gun? Is that why you had one ready to use?" Mary asked.

"No. I don't know what planet you're from, but you have no idea about normal people, do you?" Anger, hot and sudden, rose from her chest and heated her face. She was sure that even the roots of her hair were burning. "I didn't want to learn how to shoot the gun. I don't believe in taking a life for any reason. I'd never thought I'd ever need to *kill* someone. I was angry with Flick for insisting I learned in case something happened to her. I shouted at her about it. Then we got to the checkpoint and a guard came toward us holding his gun at her, and he was about to pull the trigger... I shot him." Her eyes filled and her whole body shook with the memory. "I'm going to take that moment to my grave. I don't know his name, but I do know that it was either him or Flick." Zamira needed to get her mojo back. This woman was trying to unsettle her. And she was succeeding.

Nausea twisted her stomach, and there was a buzzing in her ears. She was back at the checkpoint with the guard coming toward her, gun raised. She ducked down behind Flick as she watched the guard shoot her again and again. Zamira screamed.

"Ms. Saliev. Zamira. Zamira. Breathe. Yes, that's good. Breathe slowly and deeply. Breathe in and breathe out. You're safe. Flick is safe. Keep breathing slowly. Deep breaths." Mary knelt beside her chair, holding Zamira's hands. "You're safe. You just had a flashback."

They sat in silence for some time, the only sound was Zamira's breath in and out. She was lightheaded and so exhausted it hurt to keep her eyes open. She tried to stifle a yawn.

"Thank you for telling us about your journey. I want you to get a shower, some hot food, and some sleep. I'll take you to your room." Mary stood, gesturing for her to do the same.

She led Zamira down the corridor to a small studio room with an adjoining bathroom. On the bed was a supply of clothing and towels.

"We've put toiletries in the bathroom. There should be everything you need. I'll just organize some hot food for you, and I'll be back shortly." She turned and walked toward the door. She opened it and stopped. "I'll accompany you to eat. Please don't wander about alone. This is a secure area, and you're likely to be arrested if you do."

Zamira stood in the middle of the room and couldn't move. It was all so unreal. She knew she was on an airfield; she'd heard planes and helicopters. She'd spent the best part of a week outside, and now she was shut in again. There were no windows. She went into the bathroom and locked the door. She caught sight of her face in the mirror above the sink. She was a mess. Her hair was matted and ragged and dirty, and her face was grimy. She could easily be a street beggar in Tarinor. She tried to see the rest of her in the mirror but couldn't see much other than clothes that were dusty, dirty, and muddy in places. She stripped her clothing off and put it into a pile to be put straight in the trash.

She switched on the shower and waited for the water to heat up. Lemon-scented shampoo cut through the smell of dirt that seemed to emanate from her body. She scrubbed until her skin was raw. Once she was clean, Zamira luxuriated in the hot water and soaked her aching muscles. She let her mind go blank. For the first time in ten days, she was safe.

Eventually she turned the shower off and dried herself. She put on the underwear, T-shirt, and sweats that had been provided. They fit well enough though the socks were enormous, and the slippers were like boats on her feet. They were better than bare feet. She went through to the bedroom and tried to fix her hair. They'd provided a brush and comb, and she made a good attempt at getting most of the knots out.

There was a tap at the door. Her escort, no doubt. As much as Zamira knew she was safe, she couldn't lose the feeling of being a prisoner here until she'd told them everything she'd said and done in her time with Flick. "Come in."

Mary stuck her head in. "Ready for some proper food?" She opened the door wider, and Zamira followed her out. They went into another corridor, and Zamira wondered why the smell of food seemed to be the same in any institution in the Western world. Her university cafeteria was much like it—old grease, overcooked vegetables, and an unidentifiable mixture of herbs that didn't go well together. Mary led her into a small, empty dining room with scuffed lino flooring and plastic-covered tables for four.

"Is Flick going to join us?" Zamira asked.

"No, she's in the medical center where they're treating her gunshot wound. I don't expect she'll be released for a few days."

The thought of Flick laying alone and unconscious in a sterile room made Zamira's heart hurt. But that was Flick's life, right? It had nothing to do with her. Following Mary's lead, Zamira went to the buffet and helped herself to two slices of cheese and tomato pizza, a large portion of fries, and a large glass of cola before sitting at a table. Mary joined her, and Zamira sat silently as she ate her meal.

"What happens now?" Zamira asked finally, feeling the pizza sitting heavily in her stomach.

"We need to have a conversation about your safety and security when you get home." Mary tapped the end of her pen against the table. "It's likely that you'll still be a target. Like your father, you've been an embarrassment to the president, and he may want to remove you permanently instead of kidnap you."

Zamira regretted eating all that food. Her stomach was doing cartwheels with anxiety, and she thought she may be sick. She'd gone through all this to be back in the same tenuous position.

"In our favor, the international media are on your side, and we can make sure that they stay that way. It will help to keep you safe, certainly in the short term."

But she was currently out of sight and in a military installation. "Will I have to go into hiding? Live in a safe house and be under guard? Please tell me I won't?" Zamira shuddered as she worried about losing the life she'd worked so hard to get.

"No. We'll work out something for the future, but I'll make sure you have an armed escort home, and you can stay in your flat with an armed guard. We can organize going forward once you're in Paris."

Zamira breathed a sigh of relief. Home to Paris. Her words were comforting.

"I suggest you have a good night's sleep, and I'll pick you up from your room for breakfast in the morning. I have you scheduled on a flight to Paris, leaving at ten. I'll get you some shoes. European thirty-nine?" Mary asked.

"Yes, and can you lend me some money, please? I'll need to get home from the airport." Zamira wondered if her father knew what had happened to her. She hadn't had a chance to think about him, and her guilt gave her stomach a sinking feeling. "Has anyone told my papa what has happened?"

"Yes. Your father has been briefed and is aware that you're safe. I don't know anything else. Are you expecting a message?" Mary asked.

"No. No message. As long as he's not worrying," Zamira said. Why would he send her a message? The man who'd put his family in constant jeopardy, who hadn't quit even when they'd killed his wife. She swallowed against the old, raw anger. Why did it hurt so much and yet she could still wish he was holding her, telling her it would all be okay?

"I'll give you some money tomorrow morning. You can also make a couple of phone calls if you need to," Mary said.

They finished eating, and Mary escorted Zamira back to her room. She was exhausted and could hardly think straight. She took off her clothes and turned back the crisp, white sheets. She sat on the small bed, hurting at the contrast between the cold and brown of the ground on the plains and the warm and white of the bed in this room. She wanted Flick to hold her as she had each night they were together. She hadn't managed to see her and wondered if she should check on her. Flick had spent a lot of their time together making sure Zamira was fed, clothed, and warm. She'd taken care of her physically and mentally.

Zamira lay down and closed her eyes. They knew each other well in some things and not at all in so many others. She'd abandoned Flick because she lived a life that was held together with shadows and untruths, a life that Flick obviously loved and was good at. Flick hadn't stood up for herself when she'd called her out. That was her anguish. Her hopes and dreams for a loving relationship in Paris and London didn't mean anything to Flick. Part of her always understood that it wouldn't work. Their lives were too different. Perhaps she shouldn't have said goodbye. Had she made a mistake? No. If they couldn't talk to each other about their feelings, they weren't meant to be. She was as alone as she'd ever been since her mumma died, and she had to get used to it.

***

When Zamira boarded the plane, she wasn't certain she'd survive the flight. Her heart hammered in her chest, and it was hard to breathe. She looked around at other passengers and tried to guess if any of them were from Tarinor and worked for the president. Everyone could be a bad guy, and her hands shook as she buckled her seatbelt.

Mary had found her a pair of trainers and given her some money and an escort. She was traveling with a Marine named Joe whose sole instruction was to see her home safely. He was a muscular guy who had obviously seen action, military or otherwise, judging by his bent nose and scarred face. He smiled at her when they were introduced and had been a quiet, even presence. She liked his silence; she couldn't cope with a conversation at the moment. She slept for most of the journey, waking only when a meal was served, and she sat drowsily as they stopped in Istanbul to collect more passengers. Joe had looked at each embarking passenger carefully. It made her feel a little safer, but she couldn't help but wish it was Flick beside her, watching, keeping her calm. Every time she thought of Flick, her eyes welled up. She hadn't even said goodbye to the woman who had opened up something beautiful in her. How could such a strange, special time suddenly...end?

Before she knew it, they were landing in Paris, and she breathed a sigh of relief. She was home, back to the familiar. Joe accompanied her into the arrival hall. She had no luggage, and Joe only had a small leather satchel.

"Zamira!" someone shouted. "Zamira!"

She looked around and there, not ten feet away, was her father.

Without a thought, she ran over and threw her arms around him. His strong hug was just what she needed. She had so much time to make up, so much to talk about. Joe was right behind her, and she turned. "This is Joe, my shadow," Zamira said. Joe looked around and nodded to another man close to her father.

"Thank you for bringing my daughter back. We'll take over now," he said. He turned, and the man with him nodded a second time. "This is Daniel, my shadow. He will look after us both for a few days until I have to leave, and then we'll decide what you need."

Joe gave them a quick nod and smile. "Good luck." He turned and left without a backward glance.

"I've missed you. I'd love to spend some time with you, so I've rented a three-bed loft apartment near the Opéra underground station. You don't have to stay with us, but it's airy and spacious and will give us some time to talk and for you to adjust before going home," her father said, his expression hopeful.

"I need to go to my apartment to get some clothes and other bits and pieces. I have nothing but the borrowed clothes I'm wearing," Zamira said.

Her father hooked his arm through hers. "We'll go there first and then on to our apartment."

***

They arrived at his rented loft at ten p.m. Zamira settled into her third-floor bedroom, overlooking some gardens. It gave her a welcome feeling of security being there with Daniel and her father. She unpacked some of her things and went to enjoy a hot shower while her father ordered takeout. She thought back to that day standing at the edge of the plain with Flick, desperate for a pizza. Here she was, pizza and no Flick. Her heart ached. Had she been a coward and put all the blame on Flick? Maybe, but it was too late now.

As she stood in the shower, she thought about the strength of her father coming to meet her, despite not knowing how she might greet him. She'd lost her anger at him in the cold, harsh reality of Tarinor and realized how much she missed him. When she'd told Flick about how he spent days looking for her mother and the state of him when they'd found out she'd been murdered, she realized he was hurting as much as she was. She'd taken her pain out on him without once stopping to think about how he'd lost his beloved wife.

Her thoughts drifted as she let the water run over her body, and she couldn't help but think about Flick again. She was still angry with Flick for not wanting to take that step to explore whatever was between them. Their electricity was more than just attraction. Flick could ignore it, but Zamira was certain they had something special. She hadn't said anything to Flick about her feelings, because she didn't want to hear Flick to say she felt nothing. They'd felt so close in Tarinor, but she actually knew very little about her. She didn't know where she lived, what her real name was, in fact almost nothing concrete about her life. The water turned cold and forced Zamira out into the bathroom to get dressed.

She went into the kitchen where her father handed her a plate of pizza and some chopped salad.

"Daniel has taken his meal into his room to give us some privacy," he said. Zamira sat at the dining table, and he sat opposite her. "I've made us a cup of green tea. Is it still a favorite of yours?"

"It is. Tea was the only thing we had plenty of on the journey out of Tarinor." She had to start the conversation with her father. She'd been the one to create the rift. She'd believed him to be reckless with her mother's life, and that had set her on a path of anger. She still had a little resentment toward him, but the flame had turned to dying embers. "I'm sorry—"

He shook his head. "You have nothing to be sorry for. You may not believe this, but I understand. I've always understood why you blamed me for your mother's murder. I struggle with those thoughts myself. If I hadn't done this or if I hadn't done that. I have to tell myself daily that it's the Tarinor government that did it."

"I'm still sorry that I was so angry with you. Looking back, I can see how we were both in so much pain, but I turned away from you instead of toward you. I tried to get on with my life," Zamira said.

"Your very successful life. I'm impressed that you found a place to study and started somewhere new. I saw you were off to give a paper in Japan when you were kidnapped," he said.

"I suppose you could say that all your discussion with Mumma about what was wrong in Tarinor rubbed off. I've been studying government corruption. Although I was kidnapped because they wanted to silence you, give it a few years and it'll be me they want to silence," Zamira said. It was true, and the thought that she would carry on her father's legacy sparked something new inside her, something that burned deeper than anger and fear. She *wanted* to fight.

They began a long conversation about Zamira's studies and where they were taking her, and how he was trying to negate corruption from outside Tarinor by building awareness and getting other governments to listen. Zamira was calm and at peace. They talked as if they'd never been apart, as if it was a normal day.

"You're living in London now?" Zamira asked.

He cleared the table. "Officially, yes, but I've become a bit of a nomad. I'm much harder to keep tabs on that way. I'm working with governments in the UK, US, and Europe. I'm also working with secret services of those governments and with Interpol. Hence, your rescue." He came around the table and put his arms around Zamira. "Let's sleep. Tomorrow we can talk about what happened to you and think about how we stop it from happening again."

"Goodnight, Papa," Zamira said and went to her room. Once in bed, she succumbed to the emotional and physical exhaustion pummeling her. She was safe, she was with her father, and she didn't have to worry for a while. A deathly tiredness enveloped her, and she climbed under the covers without brushing her teeth. She hugged her pillow and was reminded of Flick's body wrapped around her. She hoped that Flick missed her. Had she thought about her yet today? Zamira had a cold and empty spot inside her that she had to get a hold of. Time could heal her, but so much had happened in those days. Flick was gone, and Zamira had her life in Paris. She hoped Flick was okay and that she was recovering well. Zamira's tears wet the pillow until she fell into a dreamless sleep.

***

In the morning, Zamira's first thought was of Flick. It would be yet another day when she wouldn't see her. Was she out of the hospital? Had she made it home yet? Hell, where *was* home? Zamira had to forget her. They'd met under extraordinary circumstances and their lives were in different worlds. She sighed and sat up in bed. Life would be flat without Flick to talk about it with, without Flick to share her days.

She joined her father and Daniel for tea and the croissants that Daniel had brought from the boulangerie across the road. Sitting at the little Formica table drinking her tea was a different world to the mountains in Tarinor, and Zamira found she wanted to tell her father the whole story. She gestured for Daniel to stay. If he was going to be protecting them, he should know the whole story too. When Zamira pulled out her necklace from under her shirt and showed him the bracelet under the cuff, her father had tears in his eyes.

He smiled. "I'm so happy that jewelry protected you. I didn't expect that. I wanted you to know that I loved you as much as I loved your mother when I gave it to you," he said. "Perhaps she was looking out for you."

She continued her story, though now it sounded almost like someone else's. Or it would have if she couldn't still feel Flick's body pressed against hers, protecting her from falling rocks and freezing to death.

When she'd finished her father held her hands. "It sounds as if we owe Flick a lot. I met her in London to beg her to rescue you. She's highly thought of," he said. "I'll thank her when I return."

"That'll be good, Papa." There wasn't much more she could say. Flick might not even be in London. Would she think of Zamira ever again? She moved on from the thoughts that had no answers. "Do you and Daniel think I need a security guard? Am I still a target?" Zamira really didn't want protection. It would be intrusive, but she didn't want any return to worries of getting captured either. Life in the prison had been devastating. She would never forget those guards and their nighttime visit. She shuddered. She'd always been quite a loner and the thought of someone with her all the while was a little overwhelming. She told herself that it would keep her safe.

"I think I ought to find someone for you in the short-term," Daniel said. "You'll be able to carry on your life knowing someone is looking out for you. It could be someone young, so they fit in with your lifestyle. What do you think, Almaz?"

"Yes, it's a good idea. We would use the same funding source that we use for you, I assume," her father said.

"I don't really have any choice, do I? I don't want someone butting into my life, nor do I want to be worried about getting kidnapped or killed," Zamira said.

"I know, darling. We need you safe. Just as I have a bodyguard, so will you have one. I just can't risk losing you again. I love you so much. And you can interview the people Daniel thinks are suitable," he said.

"Okay. I'll quit moaning. I love you too, Papa. So, what are you doing at the moment? Where are you working?"

"I have a lot of irons in the fire. Mostly, I've been putting pressure on countries around Tarinor to get them to report border aggression and incursions as a security risk and to highlight their case to the UN Security Council. It's a little difficult as I really don't want countries imposing sanctions on an already poor country. It's early days yet, but President Bek will get himself into trouble eventually."

"I hope so. Some of my study on corruption shows how important transparency is, that the population can see exactly what's happening in government and how. Not enough people know about your fight, and we need to spread the word that once the process of having power is open and visible to all, then corruption will disappear." Zamira registered her naïveté as she spoke. "I know it's a little innocent-sounding but underneath all the talk, that does need to be the goal."

"I agree, darling. I have been doing some work with several ex-Tarinor officials who've fled the corruption, and I want you to talk with them too. Maybe we can put together something that will move them forward," her father said.

Zamira clapped her hands. "Yes. I'd like that. Are you all in London?"

"I have a flat there, yes. I've sent the address to your new phone. I'm often away though, and I sleep in boarding houses and in friends' spare rooms when I'm traveling. The exiles are all over, with several in the Netherlands."

"Perhaps we can meet up in London or Holland. Now that we're together again, I'd like to spend time with you and find out more about your world." They were both still at risk from the Tarinor government, and the worry that she might lose her father could make her lose her breath.

"The job means I'm often traveling, but I really want to spend more time with you. I can come here, and we can eat far too many croque monsieur, and I can talk to your research group. We'll stay close."

Zamira could tell that he was as concerned as she was that they would still be in danger.

"Let's go and find some lunch and spend some quality time together before we have to go our separate ways."

Zamira decided to go with the flow for the moment. She had her papa with her and the prospect of a few days enjoying his company. The rest could wait.

CHAPTER FOURTEEN

IT WAS DARK AND warm, and Flick didn't want to wake up. This cocoon was safe, she had no responsibilities, and she could just be. She didn't move or open her eyes and enjoyed the moment. She was next aware she was having the same moment again, and it was still dark. She must have been asleep.

She opened grit-filled eyes to look up at a white ceiling. She was in the medical center, judging by the smell of antiseptic and polish, and her shoulder hurt.

She'd been sent straight here from the helo and hadn't had time to say goodbye to Zamira. Her final comments came back to her, and Flick sucked in a breath. Her shoulder injury made her cry with pain, but it was more than that. She'd always loved her work and getting out into the field. Meeting Zamira had changed that. Zamira was right that she was living a lie. So much of what she did was to hide herself, and it had taken Zamira to point that out. But she'd rarely told anyone but Leah the truth about her life. She'd always shaved elements of the story to hide herself in plain sight. It had never bothered her before. Did loving someone mean she needed to give up her job, the job she loved? Did she love Zamira?

The only way Flick could do anything about it was to examine what she had in her life, and once she'd taken a good look, she could change those things that weren't how she wanted them to be. She would always love Leah, that was a given. But she could now see she had the beginnings of feelings for Zamira, like new shoots in a garden. And she wanted to see if she could make those beginnings a little stronger, turn the shoots into flowers. But to do that, she needed to change some things.

"Oh, good. You're awake, lass." A doctor entered the room and walked around the bed. "How are you?"

"I've been better. My shoulder feels like an elephant stepped on it. Other than that, being starving, and my mouth feeling like the plains I walked through, I'm fine," Flick said.

"Luckily, I can help with all that. We washed out the wound, cleaned out a few fragments, and sewed it up. You'll be sore while it heals, so you'll have to take it easy for a while." She lifted Flick's good arm and took her pulse. "I want you to take pain killers for the next twenty-four hours and then we'll revisit. I'll have the pain killers brought in with some food and a drink," she said.

"Good," Flick said. "If you have fries, can I have some, please? And a glass of cold milk?"

"I think there's ham, egg, and chips. Will that work?" The doctor made some notations on a chart.

"I've hardly eaten for a few days, so that sounds perfect. Thank you." She wanted to ask about Zamira, but the doc probably didn't know anything. "Will I have full use of my arm again?"

"Amazingly, yes. You were incredibly lucky. The bullet passed through without hitting anything serious. Physical therapy should help you get full range back, but it will take time." The doctor tilted her head. "The rest of your body took quite a bashing too. We heard you were caught in a rockfall. It's going to take a while for all that damage to heal too. It's quite amazing that you weren't hurt worse."

Relief flooded through her. Recovery and PT she could handle. Not being able to use her arm would seriously mess with her ability to go on missions.

After food and painkillers, Flick got up and sat by the side of her bed, lost in a myriad of thoughts.

Mary knocked and entered. "Hey. I wasn't expecting to see you when I got to the LZ. I hope you're feeling a little better now. I didn't realize you were involved in the Tarinor kidnapping."

Flick nodded.

"I was here doing another job, but D6 asked me to debrief you and Zamira Saliev. Are you well enough to start?"

"I'm good. It's comforting to see a familiar face. Has Zamira already left?" Flick knew the likely answer but needed it confirmed.

"Yes, yesterday morning." Mary pulled up a chair.

"Did she have security?" Flick tensed as she waited for the reply. They surely wouldn't have sent Zamira back to Paris on her own.

"Yes, she had a Marine with her. Her father met her from the airport, and he has his own security, so she'll be safe," Mary said.

Flick released the tension and felt a blush rush across her face. She hoped she didn't come across as caring too much. But it was the truth. She did care, and she'd had enough of lies. "So, you'll want the usual debrief? Yes, you can record it. The documents and maps are all in the office, and Alex Hartley, my number two, will be able to give you copies if you need them," Flick said.

"Yes, please. Usual debrief, and thank you for the docs." Mary turned on the recorder and settled back to listen as Flick began.

She slowed when she reached the part about the crash. She spoke about Chalky's courage and recommended she should receive an award for her bravery. She was then silent for a moment as the ache, the smoke, the wreckage, filled her. "May I have a break for ten minutes, please? Could I get some coffee too?"

"Of course. I'll be back in a while." Mary left the room.

Flick laid on her bed and closed her eyes. She wanted someone to hold her, someone to calm the sorrow and grief. *Zamira*. She remembered Chalky and Slim and those days with Leah and tried to imagine them on the other side, together and having fun. It was the best she could do for now.

Mary cleared her throat to signal her return. Flick was pleased that she recognized her sadness by giving her some time and space but didn't feel the need to get all mushy.

"Coffee," Mary said and put the cup on her bedside table. "You can stay there if that's more comfortable."

Flick took a swig of her coffee and kept going. She got to the point where Zamira shot the guard. "It was stupid. I wasn't moving fast enough. I was field rusty. I'd sat at my desk too long and needed some real-life workouts," Flick said. Her face was hot, and she yanked threads from the blanket. "It's the kind of injury that happens to a newbie." When she was done, it was like she'd emptied herself, a dry kettle with no more water. Hollow.

"I've switched the recording off, and we can chat. Do you want more food or drink?"

"No, thanks. How's Mo?" Flick hadn't seen Mary and her wife for a few months and only a couple of times since Leah's death. They were great friends and had always been supportive of her. They were an older couple and had been through a lot of family upset to finally get together, so they were both grounded and understanding.

"Mo's good. She's still keeping everyone fed with her cakes and biscuits. She'll be pleased I've seen you. Now, tell me about Zamira Saliev."

"I just did. Everything." Flick stared at her, daring her to disagree.

"No. You told me everything I needed to know officially. But I can tell from seeing you and her together, and separately, that something is going on. So, spill." Mary stared her down.

Flick let out her breath. "Well, nothing's going on at the moment, and I'm in such a state. I want there to be something between us, but I haven't done much right to get it going." She told Mary how things between them had gone and the last talk that Zamira had with her.

Mary leaned back in her chair and put her feet on Flick's bed. "Why are you confused? It seems straightforward to me. You like the girl. Go get her."

Flick shook her head. Mary didn't understand. "You've oversimplified it," Flick said. "There's much more to it than that."

"What more is there?" Mary asked. "There's only love, and if it's true, you'll find a way."

Flick couldn't believe that. There was much more to her confusion. "I've always loved my job, and I'm good at it. When I was promoted and grieving, I felt my life pass me by. I couldn't wait to get back into the field."

"I can understand that. And now?"

"I love it. I'm good at it, but I don't know that I want it. Zamira has made me doubt myself. I haven't been able to tell her details about my work and more importantly, about me. I didn't lie as such, but I only told her small things that don't identify me. She knows nothing solid about me, and I hate that."

"Ah, that old nut. It was something you didn't have to face with Leah."

"Exactly. It wasn't a problem. We were both military and worked in the same place. We left Afghanistan and went home together. Zamira's different; she's not military."

"I don't think you've given her a chance. You expected her not to understand and that you'd probably have to give up the job you love to be with her. Perhaps if you talked to her, it wouldn't be like that."

Flick heard what Mary was saying. She hadn't stood up for herself at all. Her stomach felt empty, and her aching body grew heavy. Maybe it *was* that simple.

"Even so, I'm not sure that's the reason. Perhaps there's a part of you that hurt so much after Leah died that you don't want that hurt again. What better way to avoid that than to end this relationship now."

Flick sat upright and froze.

"You need to stop making excuses and decide if you like Zamira enough to work out a future together."

"So why am I worrying if this is the job for me? I've had enough of losing friends and colleagues. I'm sick and tired of injuries and hospitals." Her voice grew louder, and she was losing her temper.

"You're just using it all as an excuse. You really want to go find Zamira. I told you, it's simple and eventually you'll realize that." Mary stayed calm. She stood. "I'm going to leave you to your thoughts. I'll give Mo your love. Come and see us soon."

Flick pushed herself up on the bed, her body screaming. "So what's the plan with me now?"

"The medics want you to have another twenty-four hours here, and then we'll fly you to London. Is there someone at home who can keep an eye on you for a few days?" Mary asked.

"I'll contact my parents and get them to pick me up. I'll spend a few days with them," Flick said. She was battered and bruised, mentally and physically, and needed some time to regroup and think her way through the problem that was Zamira Saliev.

CHAPTER FIFTEEN

AT BREAKFAST ON FLICK'S first morning in Norfolk, she went into the dining room and found her mother reading a magazine. The room was cavernous, with flock wallpaper and a long, highly polished mahogany dining table. Her mother sat at the far end of the table, where the sunshine came in through the open French doors.

"Buongiorno, cara. How're you feeling after a night in your old bedroom? Did you manage to sleep?" her mother asked.

"Like a log. The flight home was long, and I was so tired last night. Am I too late for breakfast?" Flick stood in the sunshine.

"What do you fancy?"

Flick pulled up a chair and sat close to her mother. "I'd love a mug of strong coffee and a couple of slices of toast covered with butter—"

"I'll tell Cook and get her to bring it through." Her mother was already halfway to the door.

"And I'd also like to spend some time today talking to you about my life and what I want to do with it," Flick said.

Her mother stopped and turned toward her. "Of course. I'd love that."

She'd rarely talked to her mother about her life and her dreams. In fact, she'd rarely shared anything with her mother. Talking to Zamira had helped her realize how she'd cut her mother out of her life. She hadn't shared much of her life with her family at all, and she'd never spoken to them about being gay. She had presented Leah to them as "the woman I'm marrying next month." To their credit, they took it all in their stride, and she knew that they had cared for Leah, the little they knew of her.

Her mother returned, sat down next to Flick, and took her hand.

"I know I don't come home often these days."

"Life has been hard for you over the past couple of years, I expect," her mother said.

"I've been in a dark place since I lost Leah, and I've hardly done anything or been anywhere. I didn't want to come home with all the memories from here and the wonderful time we had in the dowager's cottage. I was living a shadow life," Flick said, tears welling up in her eyes.

"Has anything changed? I thought you'd been promoted to a desk," her mother said and then laughed. "Although not many special operatives get shot sitting in their office in the Ministry."

Their cook appeared with her breakfast. Flick had a long conversation with her about her recipe for kedgeree and her rugby-playing sons before she left to prepare lunch. It was a good way to avoid her mother's question. What *had* changed? She took a sip of her coffee and met her mother's gaze. "Alex says I've grieved enough, and I need to start living again. A job came in that I knew we wouldn't take because it was just one woman and would cost too much. But I fought for it, and it went right up to the top. Uncle Noel helped with my case, and it was approved. I was so pleased." She rolled her aching shoulder and tried to release the tension in her jaw. She took another bite of her toast which seemed to be disappearing quickly. That taste of home was irreplaceable.

"I realized I love what I do. I managed to get the woman, Zamira, out, but on the way, I learned so much about myself. Before I left, I'd become a bored manager sitting at a desk. All my training was unused, all the languages and the survival skills fading away," Flick said. "But once I was in the field, in my element, I wasn't sure that's where I wanted to be. I lost Chalky and Slim, and I ended up in hospital, and nothing seemed right. I hated not telling the truth about myself and realized it would be impossible to have a relationship with someone non-military." She leaned back in her chair and closed her eyes. She could see Zamira's eyes flashing when they clashed. She was so beautiful.

"Zamira made me think about so many things as we walked across the top of the world. Then she went back to her life, leaving me working out how to rebuild mine and how that might include her," Flick said. "If that's even what she wants."

"I wondered if there was a woman in there somewhere. Tell me about her. Where is she? What is she doing? Let's go into my study so we won't be disturbed," her mother said.

Flick followed her down the familiar hallway into the room at the end. She hadn't been in here often; she'd spent most of her time with her brothers in the estate and farm office, if not out on the estate itself. It was homely with floral curtains and a matching sofa and chairs. It smelled flowery and was a slice of her memories of her mother.

Her mother sat in one of the chairs that was obviously her regular seat. There was a pile of books and magazines on the little table next to it. She patted the chair next to her. "Tell me about Zamira."

Flick sat in the somewhat dainty chair and stretched her legs out in front of her. She didn't know where to start. This wasn't the sort of conversation she'd ever had with her mother. "She's about as tall as you, with mussed up hair and... Well, I've never seen her dressed in anything decent. She has a fiery temper, and her eyes flash when she's angry. She's beautiful and kind. She hates the idea of hurting anyone or anything, and she makes me think," Flick said. "That's not a good description. I just don't seem to have the words. She brings out this need in me... I want to protect her. I want to make her smile."

"That's good, yes?" her mother asked.

"I suppose so. But she doesn't want the me that goes with the work. She says I live a life of lies," Flick said.

"She's found you out."

"Yeah...wait. What? What do you mean?" Indignation was building up inside. She clenched her teeth. She had always rebelled against her mother and was doing it again automatically. She made herself calm down. Her mother wasn't saying anything she hadn't started to figure out for herself.

"Felicity Seraphina Hickling, you're my daughter. I love you. I have always been sad that you think you're not the daughter I wanted. I made the mistake of trying to put you in a frilly dress *once*, and you've never forgiven me," her mother said.

Flick remembered telling the same story to Zamira and smiled.

"I only ever wanted you to be yourself and to be happy. Your father always hoped that one of our children would continue the family name, but it never had to be you. We know you're unconventional as far as families like ours go, but we don't want you to change. We don't love you any less. You always thought we wanted something else and that you'd let us down. We're all happy that you are who you are. Stop trying to be another person."

Her mother put out her arms, and Flick put her head on her shoulder. She hadn't done this for so long, and she missed it. Tears welled up and for once, she didn't mind. Each tear she shed was one of the lies she'd carefully built her life upon.

Her mother gave her a handkerchief. White linen and not big enough for a blow of one nostril, but it sufficed for wiping her eyes. All her life, her mother always seemed to have one of these handkerchiefs, some with initials, some with emblems, some lace. They wiped her nose, bloody knees, cut hands, and a variety of childhood tears.

"I want to ask your advice about what to do next. I want to see if Zamira and I could have something between us. I think that would have to involve me living in Paris, where she studies. Heck, I don't know how she'll feel about it. She was pretty angry with me last time we spoke." Flick sighed. "I messed it up really badly. I couldn't decide what I wanted, so I said nothing. But then she walked away, and I knew I'd blown it."

"So why do you need my advice? It's obvious you need to go and win her back," her mother said.

"You'd be all right with me living in Paris?" Flick asked.

"It'll mean I get to see you as much as I do when you're only in London. You don't exactly spend a lot of time around here, do you, love?" There was no judgement in her tone, just gentle humor. "Norwich has an airport. Was that all you wanted to ask me?" Her mother pushed her away a little and looked into her eyes. "You look frightened. Why's that?"

"She means more to me than I expected. It's been difficult getting over Leah, and then Slim and Chalky... But I've missed her. What if she doesn't want me? How do I convince her to give me a try?"

Her mother smiled. "That's a question people have asked throughout time. I know you expect me to be able to solve your problem. But I'm only your mother and I can't. I can only say that you need to be yourself, the self that she likes. The one *you* like, the one you wake up as in the morning." She pulled Flick toward her again. "I suspect that it's the person I have here cuddled up to me. And if she says no, then you'll have to work at making sure she says yes the next time you ask her."

Flick didn't hurry to move. There were still plenty of questions, plenty of things to work through. But for now, this was enough. "I've missed you. I wish I'd done and said things differently. Can we be mother and daughter properly now?"

"We always have been, but I'm happy to provide all the cuddles in the world," her mother said. "Your father will wonder what we've been doing all morning."

Flick laughed. "When we say we've been having some mother and daughter time, he'll look at us like we've grown new heads."

She thought a lot about Leah over the next week or so as she slowly healed and attended physiotherapy appointments. She was moving on, but she didn't know how she could leave her. Zamira kept overtaking her thoughts. She had started feeling guilty about it, but words from Alex and her mother ran through her mind about starting again when she was ready. She would never *not* love Leah. But she had been using her memory as a crutch, and she needed to stand upright again and say goodbye.

She went to the memorial gardens with a heavy heart. She hadn't been here since she'd had a plaque made and planted a cream rosebush alongside it. She looked at the single blooming rose and cried. All the tears were too much, and they ran down her face like an overflowing mountain stream. She knelt before the rose bush. "Hello, my darling. I'm going to start doing what everyone has been telling me to do and start living properly again. It's been over two years. God, I've been so sad and lonely. I needed you more than I can ever say. I've been angry with myself for telling you to go. Why did I do that? If you'd stayed here, you might still be alive." She let the guilt wash over her, let it flow away with the tears that wet the gravestone. Finally, she caught her breath and settled.

She sat back on her heels. "We lost Chalky and Slim on a mountain in Pakistan. There are all these holes in my life. People-sized holes, and I can't fill them. A few years ago, we were so full of it, weren't we? We could take on the world. And we did. But today, I'm the only survivor."

Flick picked a stem from the rose bush. "I'm taking this to plant in the dowager cottage so that you'll always be close to my roots. But I've met someone, and she's already important to me. I'm hoping she'll be open to us getting together. I needed to tell you about her and my plans before I could start my new life."

Flick spent a bittersweet hour with Leah saying goodbye for a time. For the first time, she could let her feelings flow. This was right. Her chats with her mother had helped her rebuild emotionally as well as letting her bruises and wound heal. She was much lighter in her mind, knowing that she would try to win Zamira back and that Leah had let her go.

CHAPTER SIXTEEN

CLOCK-WATCHING WAS INCREDIBLY TEDIOUS. Flick's first day back was already dragging, and it wasn't even noon.

Alex knocked and came in full of smiles and joy. "Good morning, boss lady," she said. "What do we have planned for today? Can you squeeze in a quick sandwich with your number two?"

Flick laughed. "Lunch will be perfect. We can catch up. I have lots to tell you."

"Good. Mr. Saliev is at the front desk filling out the forms but will be with us shortly," Alex said as she left the room.

Within moments, Almaz Saliev was at her door. Flick stood. "Mr. Saliev—"

"Almaz, please."

"Almaz, I'm so pleased to see you. How is everything?" What she really wanted to ask was, how is Zamira? Has she mentioned me? But none of those things would be appropriate. Flick had been told that Zamira had returned to Paris and was safe, but nothing more.

"I came to say a personal thank you. A handshake won't do it. May I ask for a hug? I wasn't sure I'd ever get to see my daughter again. But thanks to you, and you alone, she's safe," Almaz said.

Before Flick could respond, she was wrapped in his arms. He was very careful around her sling. Life was getting more unusual by the minute since she'd known Zamira. It was a polite but genuine hug and meant so much more than a handshake.

"Can I make you a green tea?" Flick asked. "Or have you caught our Western ways and would prefer coffee?" She directed Almaz to a comfortable chair.

"Green tea is perfect," Almaz said. "I've been waiting for you to come back to work so that I could see you. Edward told me you'd be in today. Is that his name? We all call him the general."

Names didn't mean anything around here. Flick nodded and sat down with her tea next to Almaz.

"I want to thank you for getting Zamira home safe. I am so sorry that you lost your team in the mountains. It seems such a small word for such courage and bravery of those women. They managed to contribute to Zamira's safety. I have asked the minister to do something to make sure they are remembered. Zamira didn't know much about what happened, so I asked the general, and he gave me the details."

General Moss had no idea what the sacrifice had truly been. "Two of the women were my close friends. I didn't have a chance to say goodbye during the operation. I've been to see their families, and it's given us all some closure." Flick closed her eyes. "It's still painful though." When she opened her eyes, she could see that Almaz's face was drawn, and his lips tightened.

"I understand that pain. I expect Zamira told you I lost my wife, and I still haven't recovered. To have another chance with my daughter is a gift I never thought I'd have," Almaz said.

"How is she?" Flick asked. All this politeness was too much. She just wanted to know about Zamira.

Almaz was silent for a moment before he looked at her as if judging what to say. "She's well and back at work at the university. But I think that she's still recovering from her ordeal. Being taken prisoner and having to shoot that guard... She's a gentle soul," he said.

"Is she having panic attacks or nightmares?" Flick asked.

Almaz shook his head. "She hasn't mentioned them, but I would hazard a guess that she's not sleeping well."

"I'd like to see her. Do you think I'd be welcome?" Flick held her breath waiting for the answer. There was a moment's silence as if he was considering.

"Yes, I think you would. Are you planning on a visit soon?"

There was something in his gaze that suggested he understood her motivation.

"I need to see what Zamira has to say first, but I'm hoping for quite a long stay." Flick had no idea what Zamira was feeling or thinking. But there'd been a spark, something special, and she couldn't walk away from it. The only way to do it would be to book a flight and go. All she could do was hope that Zamira wanted it too.

After talking with Almaz about some of the work he was doing with

Interpol, the germ of an idea began to form in her mind. Perhaps working in France wasn't that much of a flight of fancy. There might be a way to do the work she enjoyed and chase the woman she wanted at the same time.

She resolved to book a flight for Friday. She'd ask for some vacation time and see what the wheel of fortune had in store for her. She went to see Moss to clear her leave and discuss ways forward for her career so that she could follow up on her possible choices in France. Her mind was made up. Even if Zamira turned her away, her career path had to change anyway. It was time.

"Good afternoon, Flick, good to see you back at work again. All is well?" he asked. "I don't often get to see you up here."

He had a pot of coffee on his desk. He lifted a cup toward Flick who nodded, and he poured and handed her a cup. The pattern seemed to match the flock wallpaper in his office and Flick smiled to herself, thinking it was funny how she noticed such little things when her adrenaline was firing on full. "Yes, sir, everything is fine. As you know, I'm fit but restricted to desk duty for a couple of months. Got to get rid of this sling too."

Moss would have okayed the medics' plan for her return to work.

"I'd like to take a few days leave from Friday if that's okay?" Flick asked.

"Of course, there's not too much on at the moment. Alex seems to have it all in hand." He looked at her, his eyebrow raised. "And?"

"Well, sir, I have a dilemma that I need to talk to you about. I want to move to France, Paris specifically, and wondered if you had any ideas about how I might be able to do that and continue working with the department?" Once the words were out in the open, her spirit lifted.

Moss put his coffee cup down with a thump. "Not an easy dilemma. Why do you want to move? Bit sudden, isn't it?"

"Yes, sir. I suppose it is. I've met someone, so you'll hear about it eventually. I want to be near Zamira Saliev, not that she knows it yet." Flick flushed, slightly embarrassed at what sounded like a whim.

"Oh." He cleared his throat. "Does her father know?"

"Yes, sir," Flick said, moving uncomfortably in her chair. Discussing Zamira with her boss was disconcerting, but the department needed to know who you were having a relationship with to ensure the safety of all concerned. "You promoted me out of the field and as you know, I spent a lot of my time wanting to get back into it."

"Well, yes, I know. That was one of the reasons I was happy to let you do the Saliev job, to get you out from your desk." He took a sip of his coffee.

"Yes, sir, thank you. It was good, and it also meant that I had time to think things through. It made me realize I need a change."

"Right." Moss looked into his coffee cup. "The change is that you want to be close to Zamira Saliev?"

"Yes, sir. Can you make France work for me, even if it's only for the next year or so, please?" Flick asked. "If you don't have anything then I'll probably have to leave, or maybe request permission to work remotely."

"I don't want to lose you, Flick. You're one of my best operatives, and we need you. We do have a few jobs coming up that will need work with the French Internal Security Agency. You're one of my fluent French speakers, aren't you?"

Flick nodded.

"Mm. And it's funny you should ask about France. I've been getting hassle about how we should be using Interpol more. We can't always be covered by our uniform friends, and our own liaison would be a good thing." Moss tapped his fingers on the highly polished oak desktop.

The rhythm reminded Flick of horse's hooves echoing around the silent room. Flick wished she could hear Moss's thoughts. He held her future in that tapping hand, and it would resolve in the space of a couple of minutes of his thoughts. Her time with the department could be over in a moment. She wondered at the number of people that had been in this position, with the boss making decisions affecting their lives in a two-minute thought process.

"Yes. Let's try this. We could create a Special Interpol and French Liaison Officer reporting directly to me in Department Six. It'll solve my problem and get everyone off my back. In addition, it'll let you sort things out in France. I'll need to come up with the job specs for the bean counters, and I'll need to clear it with the minister. I hope that might work out for you." He smiled and poured himself another coffee.

Flick could hardly hear her thoughts over the rapid beating of her heart. France was on the cards. Now all she had to do was get to Paris and convince Zamira that she could be the kind of person she wanted and deserved. When she'd first started thinking of the possibility of Zamira as a partner, the problems had seemed insurmountable. Distance, family, work... None of them were actual issues now. Flick's stomach sank. She'd gotten this far but what if Zamira wouldn't see her or didn't want her? *Suck it up, Felicity Seraphina. You're committed. Don't start getting cold feet at the final stage.* She could hear her mother's voice and it made her smile.

She became aware of Moss speaking.

"As I just said, I won't be able to offer you anything in the field and the job will mean a bit of travel," Moss said.

"That's no problem at all. I'll work it into my plans," Flick said. She didn't want Zamira to find herself a widow if Flick was lost on an op. She had survived so many, the roll of the dice was likely to come her way sooner rather than later.

There were still forces at work here making the way for her and Zamira. She booked a flight to Paris, trying to ensure that those forces stayed on her side as she counted the days until she'd see Zamira again.

CHAPTER SEVENTEEN

IT WAS ANOTHER GRAY Paris morning as Zamira looked out of her window across the grassy square surrounded by similar windows. The campus was all square boxes, devoid of the beautiful French architecture that was prevalent in the center of Paris. Her flat was basic, but she'd managed to get free accommodation from the French government when she arrived from Tarinor to study for a PhD. She shouldn't complain. She wasn't earning much money, and it would do until she started her full-time position with the research group. The school had moved her to a much prized two-bedroom flat so that her new bodyguard could be with her. It was mortifying to have to ask, but in true Parisian style, they simply found it interesting and got on with things.

The new bodyguard was something she was struggling with. The fact that she had someone with her constantly was driving her insane. She couldn't use the bathroom without her bodyguard knowing. Going out with an extra person in tow, having to tell them where she was going, and wait for them to open doors, to scan areas, to check crowds... It was too much. Not that her bodyguard was intrusive—she wasn't. She was just there. And she was there *all the time*. Daniel had found her a female bodyguard from England. Anna was older than Zamira, perhaps in her early forties. She liked her as a person; she tended to melt into the background a lot and had given Zamira suggestions when she was doing something Anna wasn't sure about. Like when she was heading into the research offices in the evening, and they were almost deserted.

It was nearly three weeks since she'd come back from Tarinor, and she'd spent over a week with her father in their rented loft. It had been full of reminiscence and reconnection, and she was hoping he would be over to see her again in a couple of weeks. Having him around kept the loneliness and heartache at bay, for which she was grateful. He was going to help sort out somewhere for her to stay once she had her PhD. Although where the money would come from, she had no idea. A flat near the university would cost her more than a month's salary when she did start work, so she'd have to continue spending her time traveling to work and enjoying the parts of Paris that she loved.

She adored the chair by the window and spent many an hour sitting in the light, often with the window open. Sometimes she'd have her laptop on her lap as she jotted down thoughts on the work she was doing. Sometimes it was a good book. But now, as was most common, she liked to sit and greet the day, look at the tops of the trees and the changing sky with a cup of green tea in her hand before going to her office.

The wind blew a cool breeze through the open window. Something about the wind and sky made her think of the high plains in Tarinor, and she was back to thinking about Flick. It seemed in the past weeks that she could think of little else. Zamira had to admit that her truth was a little slanted. And with hindsight, who was she to judge? She wasn't a hero doing such fine work that was well hidden from plain sight.

Zamira hadn't said a proper thank you or goodbye, not that she'd had much of a chance after they'd been separated. But she hadn't gotten in touch either. She'd stomped all over Flick's feelings and left. Her spiral of thoughts wasn't doing her any good, but she couldn't stop herself thinking them. That's when she wasn't thinking about the first kiss. As always when she traveled these thoughts, she was left with tears in her eyes and a sinking feeling in her stomach.

Her thoughts were interrupted by a loud knock on the door.

Anna came out of her room. "I'll get it," she said and disappeared from sight into the miniscule hall.

She was gone for more than a few moments, and Zamira wondered if she'd had another member of the press to deal with. They'd gone crazy when Zamira hadn't been trotted out in front of the camera in Tarinor again, and when it was announced she'd been rescued and was back in Paris, there'd been cameras outside the apartment for days. She'd managed to avoid them for the most part. She had nothing to say and no desire to put a target on her back once again. She looked back out of the window and waited for Anna to give her a report.

Anna stepped back into the room. "You have a visitor. I'm going out for a couple of hours to do some shopping and will be back in time for lunch," she said.

Anna never left her alone. What kind of visitor made her feel like she could? Anna went into her room and came out wearing boots and her leather jacket and left.

Zamira went toward the hall. Her papa must have decided to come earlier. The sense of loneliness began to lift. But when she turned the corner, it wasn't him. She held onto the wall to keep her knees from buckling.

"Hi, Zamira," Flick said.

Flick was leaning against the wall, smiling. Zamira looked her up and down. Her hair was neatly trimmed, and she looked fit and healthy. She was wearing a cotton, long-sleeved collarless shirt and low-slung jeans. Zamira liked this version of Flick. Very much. She couldn't think of what to say. She didn't want to ruin this moment the way she'd ruined their last meeting. Her heart beat like a side drum as she put out her hand. "Are you real?"

Flick took her hand. "Are you going to invite me in or leave me standing in the hall?"

She stepped closer, and Zamira could smell her cologne. It made her think of the power of the sea. "Come on in. It's small, so the tour won't take long. This is the lounge, kitchen and diner. My bedroom there, Anna over there, and then the bathroom." She was suddenly lightheaded. "I need to sit down for a moment."

Flick stood looking around and then stared at Zamira. "It is small," she said. Then she looked Zamira up and down and grinned. "But perfectly formed."

"Would you like tea, English breakfast courtesy of Anna, or green? I have some ground coffee too if you'd prefer." How mundane, she thought, to be asking about something like that when she wanted—

"I'd better have the green tea, please. I've had more coffee than is good for me while I plucked up the courage to come and see you," Flick said. "I asked your father for your address when he came to see me. Didn't he tell you?"

"No, he didn't." She'd have words with him when she next spoke. She concentrated on making the tea. "Please, take a seat. How are you?"

Flick briefly looked out of the window before looking back at her. "I'm better now. After we went our separate ways in Islamabad, I was taken to the medical center and put back together again. Once I'd been debriefed, I was allowed home. Physical therapy, emotional therapy—plenty of therapy. I had loads of time to think about my life and where it was going. The things you said the last time I saw you made me think." Flick turned and looked out of the window again.

Zamira walked over to the seating area with a cup of tea for Flick and put a hand on her shoulder. "I'm sorry," she said.

Flick turned. "Why are you sorry? What you said was true," she said.

"I should have thanked you for saving me properly. That was what you expected, wasn't it? That's what I should have done," Zamira said. "Instead, I told you why I didn't want to be with you while you stood there, full of pain and fatigue having rescued me and lost your two closest friends. And when you didn't reply the way I wanted you to, I walked right out of your life."

Flick gave a pained smile. "Maybe we were both to blame. I would've liked to have talked to you once I was out of the medical center, but you'd gone, and when you didn't reach out, I figured you didn't want to see me. I'm here now though, and there are some things I'd like to say. Can we talk?" she said. "Perhaps start with telling me how you are?"

"I'm well and back into finishing my PhD. My professor, the one on the plane with me when I was taken, presented my paper on my behalf so I didn't miss the deadline, and it was recorded so I got to see the questions. I'm only a couple of months away from submitting now," Zamira said. "I'll go straight into the research group while we wait for the exam, and then I'll continue." It was a simple answer. Formulaic. She'd told plenty of people the same plan. She couldn't find the words to tell Flick how much she'd missed her, how lonely she'd been, how Flick had opened a universe in her heart, and she didn't know how to explore it.

"How's Anna getting along?" Flick asked.

"What makes me think you know her?"

Flick laughed. "I do know her, and Daniel, who works for your father. They're ex-colleagues of mine from the Army. A lot of us followed similar paths, and we keep in touch."

"Anna is fine. I just hate having to have a bodyguard. I have almost no privacy and while I'm not doing anything particularly private, I do like my own space. But I don't want to be kidnapped again either."

"I understand. I expected you to have trouble accepting one. I also know you understand your father wanting to keep you safe and away from the Tarinor government, at least until things calm down a little," Flick said. Her gaze was searching, and she leaned forward slightly. "How are you feeling about what happened to you in Tarinor?"

Zamira sighed, and her shoulders slumped a little. "Half the time it seems unreal, as if it all happened to someone else and not me. It could almost be a dream. Then I remember my fear when the plane stopped, my terror when I was put in prison, and the adrenaline ride of escaping with you. If you add the shooting at the checkpoint, it isn't a dream. It's a nightmare." Her body tensed as she relived it all.

Flick pulled her chair over so that she was closer to Zamira and put her hands on Zamira's knees. "It's a lot for your mind to process, and a continual feeling of fear and terror is a lot to let go of. Don't be frightened to see one of those therapists they gave the details for," she said.

Zamira hadn't plucked up the courage yet. When she couldn't get to sleep or was having bad thoughts in the early morning, she vowed to do something about it. But once the day started, she shrugged it off as being weak. "Have you been?"

"Yes. We have to following our debrief. It's regs. Even if the op is routine, there are still things we can't let go of," she said.

Zamira wanted Flick closer. She was here. She'd come to her, and the feeling of safety that slid over her skin like silk nearly made her cry.

Flick coughed and pushed her chair back. "I came to see you for a reason, and I asked Anna to give us some space so that we can have a proper talk." She folded her hands in her lap and stared at them. "I was attracted to you when we were walking across the plains, even when you made me angry. And I didn't want to be. I worried that you were attracted to me because I rescued you. I was almost ready to move on from Leah but losing Chalky and Slim in the crash and talking about Leah made me doubt myself. In short, I was a mess," Flick said. "Is that making any sense?"

Zamira waited for Flick to let her down gently and say goodbye. It wasn't what she wanted but Flick obviously wasn't in the same space. "Yes, it makes sense. Would you like another drink before you go?"

"What? Um, no, thanks. You want me to go? I'm sorry you feel that way. I was hoping that we could perhaps get together and see where this," Flick pointed between the two of them, "is likely to go." Flick stood and headed toward the door. "I guess I thought maybe you felt the same. I should've known it was just because I was getting you out of a bad situation." She shoved her hands in her pockets. "I'm sorry. I won't bother you again."

"No. That's not what I want," Zamira's voice was too loud, and she was getting cross with herself. She was nervous and saying all the wrong things. She still hadn't told Flick how she was feeling. "I want to spend time with you too. I want to talk to you about the last few weeks. I want to talk to you about life. Most of all, I want you to hold me. I've missed you so much. Please don't go."

Flick held out her arms and Zamira moved in, allowing Flick to envelop her. They stood motionless for some time. Zamira breathed deeply and allowed herself to sink into that feeling she'd never really had: safe and cared for. Flick would protect her.

Flick leaned in, and Zamira looked up before they kissed. It was a gentle touching of their lips, much like their first kiss. Zamira reached up and pulled Flick down toward her, moving deeper into it. Flick responded, pressed against her, and set her body on fire. Eventually, they parted.

Flick led her back to the couch. "We need to work some things out. I'd like to be in Paris to date you and to try being a couple. Is that what you want?"

"What I want? Of course that's what I want. We need to be together. I'd volunteer to come to London, but this research group is world-class, and I just fit with them. I don't know if I could make it work in London—"

"There's no need for you to leave Paris. I'll have to go back to London quite often, and my parents would like to meet you." Flick smiled. "I told my mother all about you. I realized I was always worried about not being who they wanted me to be. I thought they wanted Lady Felicity Seraphina Hickling to be a girl who fitted in with estate life and the gentry. But it turns out, they just wanted me to be happy and to be whoever I wanted to be and go wherever life took me."

"Lady who? You're some kind of aristocracy?" She shook her head. "We'll definitely get back to that. For now, how will you be able to stay in Paris?" Zamira didn't dare believe this was going to be possible. "What about all your missions?"

"I'm trying something new. I have a job here with my department." She kissed Zamira's knuckles. "When I explained that I needed to live in Paris so I could follow my heart, they created a new position just for me."

Zamira feared that if she spoke at a normal level then the bubble would burst, and her dreams would float away on the breeze. "You'll be able to live here?" she whispered.

"You remember my mother's family are Italian?" Flick asked, and Zamira nodded. "They were European industrialists in the last century. They're wealthy and own houses in London, New York, and Paris." She flinched, and her gaze became wary. "Please don't think I'm some kind of snob. I was just born lucky."

"All I care about is being with you. If we stay here in this flat or in a castle on a ridge, I don't care as long as I'm with you. The fact that you do this work when you clearly don't have to says more about you than any title you might have."

Flick had made plans, changed her life, all to be near Zamira. Her heart felt like it could explode.

"I spoke to my mother about my plans for living in Paris, and she spoke to my uncle. He's offered me a furnished flat on the Left Bank in one of their houses for a peppercorn rent if I want it. I've said yes. and I slept there last night. I think you'll like it," Flick said, and her smile made her eyes crinkle in the most beautiful way. "All that's left is for me to ask you to come out with me for lunch."

"Yes, please. Unless you have any ideas, I know just the place for lunch. They have rabbit and goat on the menu this week," Zamira said, trying unsuccessfully to keep a straight face.

"I'm never going to be allowed to forget that, am I?" Flick pulled her into an embrace and kissed the top of her head.

"No way. It's how our romance started. Can we go and see your flat afterward? I want to carry on this romance in a bit of privacy. Can we tell Anna you'll take over her duties for the rest of the day?"

Flick laughed, and the sound made Zamira's soul sing.

***

Zamira's second surprise of the day was that Flick had wanted to visit her university office. Zamira was happy to take her. It was Saturday, and there'd be few people there to disturb them. She timed it so that they could go to lunch before going on to Flick's apartment. Her office was quiet, as she had hoped, and she didn't intend to linger long. She shared it with three other students, who were all at their desks. She waved and they left, only to bump into her professor in the corridor.

"Claudine, may I introduce you to Flick Colonna, my girlfriend and rescuer from Tarinor. Flick, this is Professor Claudine Treego, my supervisor, and the colleague on the plane with me when I was removed in Tarinor." The word girlfriend had slipped out. Was it too soon? Based on the way Flick squeezed her hand, it was fine.

"I'm pleased to meet you, Flick. I've heard a lot about you and your white horse. I didn't realize about the girlfriend part though," Claudine said.

Flick coughed. "The girlfriend part is something new and wonderful."

She blushed, and Zamira noted her embarrassment and how her eyes sparkled. Zamira would keep the look in her memory forever. It was a look of wonder and joy, maybe even the beginnings of love.

"I thought you were English, but I can't tell by your French accent. Are you going to be living here?" Claudine asked.

"That's the plan," Flick said.

Zamira wanted to get them to lunch and then to Flick's apartment. Standing here making polite conversation wasn't moving them toward that. She checked her watch. "We should get moving. We have an appointment."

Flick barely blinked, but a small grin touched her lips.

Claudine looked between them and laughed. "Enjoy your *appointment*," she said and went back into her office.

Over lunch, they talked about Flick's injuries and physiotherapy program, and Zamira told her about the difficulties she'd had when she'd returned, especially when it came to being startled by loud noises. Flick listened attentively, as she always had.

Following lunch near the university, they walked to Flick's flat. Zamira was astounded. It was in an expensive area in a classic French block within easy reach of a metro station. The décor for the flat was lived-in. Although it was modern, it wasn't one of those minimal furniture looks. The entrance hall had a collection of coats, umbrellas, and shoes that obviously weren't Flick's. The lounge had a couch with a high back and plumped-up cushions that could fit someone taller than Flick lying flat out. Zamira's whole flat would fit in the lounge. She turned in a slow circle, taking it all in.

"I know," Flick said. "I'm lucky. That's part of the reason I struggled with my family. People work hard to earn enough to get things, and sometimes despite all that work, they'll never get what they want. I always hated that I have a wealthy family and that I had everything without working for it. But for the first time in my life, I'm not turning something down. I need this. *We* need this." Flick lifted Zamira into her arms and sat on the sofa with Zamira on her lap.

Zamira looked into Flick's eyes and was transfixed. Her heart almost stuttered. She needed this woman to make her world show itself in full color. Without her, Paris had been muted and gray. She ran her tongue over Flick's lips, and the kiss quickly became deeper, more desperate. Flick eventually drew back, and Zamira drew a deep breath. "That was a mighty kiss," she said, trying to draw in more air.

Flick held her as if she were porcelain. She smiled, and Zamira shivered. Their being together felt right, like two pieces of a jigsaw interlocking to create a whole picture. Zamira ran her fingertips over Flick's moist lips, which were slightly swollen from the kisses. "Can we talk about this?"

Flick didn't stop smiling as Zamira continued touching her mouth and nodded.

"I'm loving the kissing and cuddles," Zamira said.

Flick held onto Zamira's hand and stopped her motion. "But?" Flick stopped smiling. "Is there a problem?"

Zamira leaned and kissed Flick gently. "No, there's no problem, as such," she said. "But I'd like us to take some time getting to know each other. I think there's more than a small spark between us, and there are enough hot embers for us to dive into sex together."

Flick looked relieved and laughed. "I'm with you on the embers. I keep pulling us apart, because I get close to you and all rational thought escapes me," she said. "Each time our bodies touch, I'm fanning those flames." She waved a hand.

Zamira nodded and smiled. "And as much as I want to leap into bed and have hot passionate sex with you, and believe me, I think it will be hot and passionate, I want to take my time. I want to believe that the time we've spent together so far has brought us much closer than the average couple, and I want this to work."

Zamira kissed her again, and they fell into each other's arms as if they'd been apart forever. When Zamira next noticed the world outside Flick, it was getting dark outside. "Do you fancy a walk along the Seine and then perhaps some food along the Left Bank?" Zamira turned back to nuzzle

Flick. Although she didn't want to disturb their closeness, she was hungry and wanted to show off part of her adopted home.

"Sure," Flick said, straightening her shirt from where Zamira had been exploring. "It'll be good to see some of romantic Paris with you," she said. "We can come back here for a drink afterward. Will you stay tonight?"

Zamira wasn't sure she could trust herself or that they could trust each other if she stayed. But she didn't want to leave Flick when she'd just found her again.

"From your silence, I take it that's a no?" Flick took her hand. "That's fine. I'll take you home at the end of the evening. I'm okay with that. Obviously, I want you here with me, but I can respect your desire to take our time."

"No. I want to stay. I was thinking how I don't want to be apart from you, having just found you again."

"You can have the second bedroom, and I promise I'll be on my best behavior. I have a spare T-shirt you can sleep in and enough overnight essentials for us both," Flick said.

"I don't know why we should worry. We managed in Tarinor," Zamira said, remembering the smell as she stepped into the shower in Islamabad. "The state of our clothes when we made it to the base...ugh. Most of mine didn't start off particularly clean either." She held her nose, and Flick laughed.

"The smell and the pain are wrapped up in a neat little package I'll never forget," Flick said. "Let me just go and talk to Anna and tell her I'll protect you overnight. She can come back tomorrow. Then lead me to food. All this kissing is making me hungry."

Zamira had never been so happy. Flick had made her feel safe and secure and loved, and that was before they'd had sex. She wanted it to be something special. Their first time together could only happen once. They'd found each other, and the spark between them had blossomed quickly despite not knowing each other well. Zamira wanted some time to get to understand the Flick that she was having growing feelings for.

CHAPTER EIGHTEEN

FLICK OPENED HER EYES, and in those first moments between the dream world and the real world when thoughts are unclear and the air is misty, she wondered where she was. Under her back was warmth and softness. There were sheets smelling as only laundered sheets can, with a morning scent. She could feel warm air moving, perhaps breath, as it blew across her chest. She couldn't move one arm that was around a warm body.

Zamira. Paris. She smiled.

She didn't move and just let her thoughts run through yesterday. This was all meant to be. There was a certainty about how the events had fallen her way. She was frightened when she'd spoken to her parents about her life and what was going wrong and how she needed to change it. They'd been surprisingly loving and helpful. It had been her twisted thinking that had caused so much trouble, and despite that, her parents loved her unconditionally. Her brothers had teased and joked with her, and she'd been invited to the next big family gathering. She didn't want to miss it.

"Where are your thoughts?" Zamira asked, her voice croaky.

She turned sideways toward a sight that she could look at every morning for the rest of her life. Zamira, with her long, beautiful hair fanned out over her pillow, resting her head on one elbow, and looking at her lips with longing.

"Eyes up here, madam," Flick said.

Zamira moved to look into her eyes, almost lazily. Flick was fascinated with how Zamira looked at her. "You remind me of one of Ocean Coco's poems." She recited it from memory:

> it's not just the beauty of her eyes
> when she gazes into mine
> it's not just the beauty of her smile
> when she sees me
> how it shines

it's not just the beauty of her touch
so soft, gentle, fine
it's not just the beauty of her kiss
that arouses into bliss
complete and total rapture
tightly holding my heart in capture
it's the beauty of her heart
that can transfix

it's the beauty of her soul
that to me
does all this

Zamira was silent for a moment. "That's beautiful. Do you think like that?"

"Well, they're Ocean's words, but they mirror my feelings exactly and say it much better than I ever would."

Zamira's eyes moved across Flick's face and her lips, inspecting every feature and blemish as she went. Using her free hand, she turned Flick's head slightly to the side. Flick could feel warmth in her ear and the sound of Zamira's breathing before her lips gently explored her lobes. It made her shiver with a whole gamut of feelings from need, want, and passion to tenderness and love. Zamira made Flick feel as if she'd swallowed a thesaurus of words and a book of love poetry.

Later that day, after some time spent discussing things they wanted to see and do together, it was coming to that point when Zamira was going to have to return to her flat. Flick dreaded it and wanted to discuss it, but she was worried she was being too possessive. She wasn't sure how to broach the subject. Moving in was too soon, but she wanted to be honest.

She lay on the sofa with her head in Zamira's lap. Zamira was reading an article on her phone on one of the beaches they said they wanted to go to. In the end, she took a deep breath and went for it.

"You're supposed to be going back to your flat in an hour or so," Flick said.

"Mm. And so?" Zamira put down her phone.

"I don't want you to go. I want you to stay. Will you move in with me?"

Flick sat up and stroked Zamira's face. "When I came to Paris to see you, I expected I'd have to work hard at getting you to accept me and was expecting to date you for months. But we're in a different place altogether. I know it's too soon. Tell me it's too soon and we should just spend the weekends together. Tell me we should be sensible."

Zamira leaned into her touch but stayed silent.

Flick had said too much and was cross with herself for pushing. "I'm sorry—"

"Don't be sorry. I was thinking the same thing and wondering how to ask you. I know I'll miss you if I go, and for you to be here and me not with you seems foolish. Yes, it may be too soon, but I don't want to leave you again." Zamira leaned further forward and pressed her lips to Flick's. She sat back. "You do realize Anna will have to move in with me, and it may cramp our style."

"She can have the third bedroom. It's enormous, so it'll be like a studio for her. We can sort it out, but she may need earplugs at some point." Flick gave her a salacious grin and Zamira blushed.

***

The following weekend, they moved Zamira's belongings into the apartment and set Anna up in the third bedroom. Zamira used her bedroom for an office to allow her to work at home and to be able to concentrate on her reading when needed. She spent the nights curled up in Flick's arms in her bed. When she'd spent her first night at the flat in the second bedroom, she'd had trouble sleeping and had asked Flick to cuddle her as they had in Tarinor. After that, Zamira hadn't gone back to the second bedroom at all, and the nightmares and sleepless nights following Tarinor seemed to be a thing of the past.

It was early Sunday morning, and they had the apartment to themselves as Anna had gone to visit friends in London for the weekend. Flick lay in bed, enjoying the moment with her arm around Zamira, who was curled into her side with her head on her shoulder.

She closed her eyes and was in that half-waking, half-sleeping place when she felt warm fingers exploring her body underneath her T-shirt. She held her breath. Zamira's fingers continued their exploration across the top of her body and slowly moved lower. Flick could no longer stay motionless. She slid her hand across Zamira's back and the other across her face and neck. Her silky skin shivered under Flick's touch.

Her hand brushed Zamira's breasts, and she both felt and heard Zamira's intake of breath. They continued their dance together, sharing the moment, building toward something deeper, something beautiful.

This was the moment that Flick had been waiting for. She'd decided that she needed to tell Zamira that she was in love with her, but there had never been the right moment. She'd also listening to another cry of "too soon" from her inner self. But honesty was everything, and she didn't want to fall back into the Flick who lived a lie, not with Zamira.

"Have I told you yet today that I love you?" she asked.

Zamira raised her head and looked into her eyes. "No, you haven't, but then I haven't told you today that I love you either."

"Really?"

"Yes, really." Zamira continued her journey across Flick's body. "Now stop talking and let me demonstrate that love."

"Properly demonstrate?"

"Can we?"

Flick pressed her lips to Zamira's in response, and they spent the next few hours exploring, entwined in each other, intent on showing each other their love. It was everything and more. Flick slid her fingers through Zamira's hair, lingered over her breasts, and breathed in her soft, sweet cries of pleasure. Magic flooded the room, and she fell into it willingly. In return, Zamira's touch set her on fire, made her arch into it, leaving her boneless and satiated.

This was love. This was what it meant to want to share herself with someone. She wanted Zamira to have all her mismatched bits and pieces. She wanted her to see the whole picture, not just things she showed the rest of the world. She pulled her closer and knew that this was the world she wanted, always. Too soon meant nothing. It could all be taken away in a blink. They both knew that firsthand. Time was so precious, and she wanted to make the most of it with Zamira.

***

The following Saturday they took a romantic sunset boat trip. The weather had been perfectly warm and the skies clear. Flick had packed a hamper of small bites and a bottle of champagne, and they'd spent much of the trip in each other's arms.

She wanted to keep these feelings for the rest of her life. She had peace in her mind for the first time in years. She knew she was loved and that she and Zamira had an honesty between them that made her safe and whole.

"Are you enjoying being romanced?" Flick asked, putting her hand on Zamira's cheek and moving along her jaw. They were facing the setting sun and bathing in its golden light. The shadows it threw were long and dark and gave Paris a fantasy air.

"Mm." Zamira kissed Flick gently.

Flick pulled back a little. "You deserve romancing for all the goodness and love you've brought into my life. I want to romance you for the rest of my life." She reached into her pocket and pulled out the amber, diamond, and gold ring she'd had commissioned. "Will you marry me?"

Zamira was still enough for Flick to have a moment's panic.

"Yes, yes, yes," she finally said, her eyes welling with tears.

Flick took Zamira's hand and put the ring on her finger. The amber and gold was in remembrance of her Lyulli necklace and the place where they had met, and the diamond represented her forever love. "I chose this ring as a symbol of my love for you. You've given me back my life, and I'm looking forward to spending every day of it with you."

Those words were the biggest truth of Flick's life so far. The days of gray and barely existing were long gone. Zamira Saliev had gotten under her skin, had taken root, and she couldn't shake her loose. Life was good.

EPILOGUE

THEY HAD DECIDED TO get married in the remains of a castle near the estate. Zamira had laughed when Flick's mum, Isabella, had suggested it, thinking of a castle from fairy tales with perhaps a turret missing. She and Flick went to visit the castle, and all that was left were a few walls of varying heights, and some had been fashioned into an area that made it an ideal wedding venue. It had a really historic feel to it. Some parts of the floor were still visible, and in one wall was a bread oven. The whole three-acre site was grass-covered, and as they stood hand in hand, the sun began to set and passed a golden glow over the walls.

"Your mother is very clever. I love this place," Zamira said. She could see their shadows stretching out across the grass in the evening sunlight.

Flicked drew her into her arms and kissed her slowly and gently. "I love it too. It'll make our vows so special to be somewhere so historic and romantic," she said. "I already feel married to you." She bent and kissed Zamira again. "You understand me and know the real me. There aren't many people that can say that. I feel safe in your arms when you hold me."

Zamira came back to the present as she stared into her reflection in the full-length mirror, amazed at how her life had changed over the last year, and took in her wedding dress.

"You look beautiful, and I'm sure that Flick will think so too," said Duchess Isabella as she appeared at her side in the mirror.

They were a similar height and coloring, and Zamira could easily be mistaken for her daughter. That her daughter, Flick, was over six feet tall surprised many people. Isabella had given birth to four children that all had her husband's height gene.

Isabella put her arm around Zamira and looked at her closely in the mirror. "It's a big day with so much going on, but I'm so pleased that you and I are here together at this moment."

"Believe me, Isabella, I'm so pleased you're here too. I've not had Mumma here to help me, and I've struggled at times, wondering what she might have wanted. But you understood, and I've appreciated your advice and help with picking out a dress and all those little things Flick wouldn't think of." She laughed, and Isabella laughed with her. They often had a small joke at Flick's expense.

"I always wanted a daughter to discuss fashion with, and I only threatened to get Flick into a dress once. She just wasn't interested."

"I know. She told me when we were walking across Tarinor." Zamira shivered despite the warmth of the English summer day. It was over a year ago but in some ways, it was still like yesterday. Her therapist had told her that she would keep the memories, but they wouldn't come back so often, nor be so debilitating. And today was her wedding day, so she wasn't going to let the past rule the present.

She looked into the mirror again, the mirror with the delicate silver frame that was probably a family heirloom and worth thousands. She was still getting used to the fact that Flick was a lady and her mother a duchess, and that they lived a different life to the one she'd been used to. She and Flick dipped in and out of the family as they continued to live in Paris, although the dowager cottage on the estate was Flick's home.

"It's certainly been a year for you, hasn't it?" Isabella said, as if she'd read her thoughts. "Both your lives have changed, certainly Flick's has. And for the better. It's been good to see her so much in love and so settled."

"Yes, it's been an amazing year. I thought leaving Tarinor when my mother died was a big change in my life. It gave me my independence. But when I met Flick, I realized that I could be both independent and dependent at the same time. That time in Tarinor and the months since has made me realize just how much I need her, every day." A familiar feeling of lightness expanded in her chest; it was the same feeling she had whenever she thought of Flick. "I shouldn't be having this conversation with my future mother-in-law."

Isabella came around and stood in front of her. "I've been waiting to have this conversation with you, and today is perhaps the best day to have it. I am sure your mother is watching you every step of the way, particularly today. Most brides think of their mother on their wedding day if they don't have them with them. I'll leave you later for a while so you can have some time with her. I just wanted you to know that I think of you as my second daughter, and I hope you can start to think of me as your second mother. If you ever feel you need to, please call me Mama."

Isabella put her arms around her, and Zamira's eyes filled with tears. She'd started thinking of Isabella as an honorary mother and was happy that they were so close and that the feelings were mutual. "Thank you, Isabella, I will do that."

There was a gentle tap at the door. "The cars have arrived, ma'am."

"Well, should we stop being maudlin? I love you. You are beautiful. Enjoy your day. Come down when you're ready. I'll go chat with your father and then head off to the church."

And suddenly Zamira was alone. She touched her bracelet and necklace and thought of her mother. She felt her mumma with her every step of the way in her life and hoped she would like to watch her marry the woman she loved. She closed her eyes and briefly gave a word of thanks.

She went down the stairs of the cottage and into the lounge where her father was pacing. He stopped suddenly when he saw Zamira.

"Darling, you look lovely. I wish your mumma was here to see this. She would have been full of tears of happiness. You make me such a proud father."

"Papa, I'm so happy. I wish Mumma was here to share the day too, but I know she's here with us in spirit. This last year has been so good for us all. Maybe my time in Tarinor was something I'll never forget but without it, I'd never have met Flick and fallen in love. I'd still be angry with you, and we would never have gotten back together."

Her father leaned forward and took her hand. His morning suit made him look handsome and somewhat stiff.

"Is your suit comfortable?"

"Yes, but it makes me feel as if I have a rod up my back. I have to hold my head high."

"Well, you should. The work we've been doing to rid Tarinor of corruption would have made Mumma so proud of you. Doing the right thing and creating an organization. The added bonus is that I've been able to get involved. And now President Bek has gone, it has become easier."

"It's good to allow the people to have a say in their government. I don't know how it happened, but when I heard Bek had been assassinated and that a number of members of his government had left the country, I was happy. I'm not sure which country pushed to remove him and his cronies, but I'm not sorry. I don't think that the country under new leadership will suddenly be better, but they are all little steps."

Zamira heard the car drawing up outside. "Let's think about today and the wonderful woman I'm about to marry," she said, taking her father by the hand and drawing him toward the door.

"I'm glad you're wearing the Lyulli necklace and bracelet. It means a lot to me, and although your mumma didn't get to wear it many times, I know she loved it."

"It has a lot of meaning for me too. After Mumma died, it held her memory for me, which is why I didn't take it off." She touched it, feeling the warmth of the amber. "It will always remind me of my time with Flick at the beginning. It was the start of something really good."

***

Zamira stood with her father at the entrance to the castle, her heart singing. It was a warm English summer day with a slight breeze blowing the air from the ripening wheat and barley fields, smelling of summer. Zamira could see Flick's brothers standing around her, their hands in their pockets, laughing. Peter, closest to Flick in age and looks, stood out in his army uniform. He was punching her arm, none too gently, and Zamira would take that picture as a memory of the day. The boys all together. Among them, with blond hair and rake skinny, was Flick's best woman, Alex. Alex had taken over for her in the office, and she and Flick had stayed close.

Flick was wearing a tailored, cream suit with a cream vest and navy shirt. She turned as if she'd felt Zamira looking at her. The world stopped spinning. There was nothing except Flick's eyes looking at her. If you could describe them as smoldering, then Zamira would do so. There was love and adoration too.

The small number of guests settled in their seats, and Flick's brothers calmed and took their places. Alex, in a contrasting navy tailored suit, stood with Flick and turned to Zamira, giving her a big smile and a nod. She set off down the aisle on the arm of her father, trying to remember every moment. Claudine sat with her research group contingent and waved and blew her a kiss. They had become firm friends, and Claudine was helping her to get her own professorship.

Then she was only a step away from Flick, who turned and held out her hand. She took it and felt the jolt of energy and love that always accompanied their touch. This was the official beginning of their life together. The words that they were about to say would only be a formal seal on their love. She was home safe, secure, and loved.

What's Your Story?

Global Wordsmiths, CIC, provides an all-encompassing service for all writers, ranging from basic proofreading and cover design to development editing, typesetting, and eBook services. A major part of our work is charity and community focused, delivering writing projects to under-served and under-represented groups across Nottinghamshire, giving voice to the voiceless and visibility to the unseen.

To learn more about what we offer, visit: www.globalwords.co.uk

A selection of books by Global Words Press:
Our Pride: with the Nottingham and Nottinghamshire ICS/NHS
Desire, Love, Identity: with the National Justice Museum
Times Past: with The Workhouse, National Trust
World At War: Farmilo Primary School
Times Past: Young at Heart with AGE UK
In Different Shoes: Stories of Trans Lives

Self-published authors working with Global Wordsmiths:
E.V. Bancroft
Valden Bush
Addison M Conley
Emma Nichols
Dee Griffiths and Ali Holah
Helena Harte
Lee Haven
Dani Lovelady Ryan
Karen Klyne
AJ Mason
Robyn Nyx
Simon Smalley
Brey Willows

Other Great Butterworth Books

Nero by Valden Bush
Will her destiny reunite her with the love of her life?
Available from Amazon (B09BXN8VTZ)

Let Love Be Enough by Robyn Nyx
When a killer sets her sights on her target, is there any stopping her?
Available on Amazon (ASIN B09YMMZ8XC)

Lyrics of Life by Brey Willows
Sometimes the only way to heal someone's heart is a song from you own.
Coming June 2023 (ISBN 9781915009265)

An Art to Love by Helena Harte
Second chances are an art form.
Available from Amazon (ASIN B0B1CD8Y42)

Of Light and Love by E.V. Bancroft
The deepest shadows paint the brightest love.
Available from Amazon (B0B64KJ3NP)

The Helion Band *by AJ Mason*
Rose's only crime was to show kindness to her royal mistress...
Available from Amazon (ASIN B09YM6TYFQ)

Caribbean Dreams by Karen Klyne
When love sails into your life, do you climb aboard?
Available from Amazon (ASIN B09M41PYM9)

That Boy of Yours Wants Looking At by Simon Smalley
A gloriously colourful and heart-rending memoir.
Available from Amazon (ASIN B09HSN9NM8)

Judge Me, Judge Me Not by James Merrick
A memoir of one gay man's battle against the world and himself.
Available from Amazon (ASIN B09CLK91N5)

LesFic Eclectic Volume Three edited by Robyn Nyx
Download direct from BookFunnel for free!

CPSIA information can be obtained
at www.ICGtesting.com
Printed in the USA
BVHW030846281122
652926BV00012B/189

9 781915 009289